Paul Marlowe

Ether Frolics

Nine Tales from the Etheric Explorers Club

SYBERTOOTH INC

SACKVILLE, NEW BRUNSWICK

Litteris Elegantis Madefimus

This work is entirely fictional. Any resemblance to real persons, places, or events, is coincidental or fictionalized – particularly the bits about the author.

First published 61 Elizabeth II (2012) by   Sybertooth Inc.
                                                   59 Salem Street
                                                   Sackville, NB
                                                   E4L 4J6
                                                   Canada
                                                   www.sybertooth.ca

The paper in this edition is acid free and meets all ANSI standards for archival quality; see the publisher's website for information on the paper's sustainable forestry & forest stewardship certification.

Magazine publication history:

"Ten Golden Roosters" was first published in Issue №3 of *Forgotten Worlds* (Scotland); "A Visit from Prospero" was first published in Issue №10 of *Andromeda Spaceways* (Australia); "The Mud Men of Tower Tunnel" was first published Issue №8 of *Forgotten Worlds* (Scotland); "Cotton Avicenna B iv" was first published in Issue №13 of *Something Wicked* (South Africa); 'The Incident at the 27th Meeting" was first published in Issue №1 of *The Willows* (USA); "66° South" was first published in Issue №2 of *The Willows* (USA); "The Resident Member" was first published in Issue №7 of *Something Wicked* (South Africa).

Library and Archives Canada Cataloguing in Publication

Marlowe, Paul, 1969-

            Ether frolics : nine tales from the Etheric Explorers Club / Paul Marlowe.

ISBN 978-0-9864974-8-3

        I. Title.

PS8626.A757E84 2012   C813'.6   C2012-901536-9

Reviews of Paul Marlowe's YA novel *Knights of the Sea*

"Paul Marlowe's style of humor is reminiscent of Neil Gaiman's lighter works ... if you enjoy dry wit, Victoriana/steampunk elements, and plucky teenagers saving the world, you'll probably like *Knights of the Sea*. It's an tale of high adventure that takes a humorous look at... well, pretty much everything, from politics to romance to lycanthropy. Give it a shot if you liked *Stardust* or *Good Omens*."

- Kelly Lasiter, *fantasyliterature.com*

"Full of humor and references to classical literature, this Victorian tale will appeal to action/adventure lovers as well as those who like a bit of fantasy thrown in ... Fun reading that will delight fans of Phillip Pullman..."

- Lois McNicol, *TriState Reviews*

"The quirkiness reminds me of Sue Townsend's Adrian Mole series, only with a lot more at stake, say, than the embarrassment of a trip to the ER following unsuccessful glue-sniffing. This is not to say Marlowe doesn't land Elliot in embarrassing situations. At least Adrian didn't also need to de-fuse bombs, or associate with suffragettes, German submarine pilots, werewolves, and the Canadian Minister of Justice ... The characters are all spot on, from one improbable moment to the next. Marlowe's offbeat humor can even be found in parts of the book where it's least expected".

- Janette King, *Historical Novels Review*

"... the novel has multiple compelling features. It is a fast-paced blend of action-adventure, fantasy and historical novel, with the added elements of erudition, humour and wit. Marlowe's style is reminiscent of 19th century literature, yet timeless enough for a 21st century reader to grasp ... Subtly and cleverly, author Paul Marlowe educates readers about the politics and preoccupations of late 19th century Canada."

- Ruth Latta, *CM Magazine*

Reviews of Paul Marlowe's YA novel *Sporeville*

"Fast paced, action-packed, and an insane blend of historical, science, fantasy, and Gothic fiction this is an excellent first book in the *Wellborn Conspiracy* series, and I sat down and inhaled this novel in a single sitting...This book is classified as "Steampunk," and if you're not sure what that is, read the definition later – it's the BOOK you need to read. Go. Run, don't walk."

- *Readers' Rants blog*

"Fans of Philip Pullman's *His Dark Materials* trilogy will certainly enjoy this novel. In fact, readers who like Gothic literature, science fiction,

fantasy, and history will all relish this book... I cannot wait for the sequel...It was absolutely the best, most delicious thing I have read in some time."
- *Resource Links* (*Sporeville* was selected for *Resource Links* magazine's 2007 Year's Best list)

"I recommend this mystery for teens who enjoy a Gothic feeling read... the times described, and the mystery, is similar to the feel of Philip Pullman's *Sally Lockhart* mysteries."
- *Mad Tales blog*

"The general teen reader will be interested by this story, for it illustrates the past with a steady hand, and carves intrigue well...anyone past double-digits can read this and enjoy it."
- *ReaderViewskids.com*

"*Sporeville* is an exciting, well written, fast paced story which captures the atmosphere of the times."
- *Historical Novels Review*

"Anyone who loves science fiction, mystery, or history will enjoy this read, which is a great novel on its own as well as a terrific start to the *Wellborn Conspiracy* series."
- *What If?* Magazine

Reviews of Paul Marlowe's short fiction

"...an entertaining and thoughtful story."
- *SciFi UK* (reviewing "The Mudmen of Tower Tunnel")

"Gritty and realistic, Marlowe achieves his goal with deft prose stokes and clever dialogue."
- Marshall Payne, *Tangent* (reviewing "Night of Sevens")

"The story is optimistic without appearing naïve, and offers a complex treatment of difficult political and economic questions. The touch of humor remains light and kind."
- Ekaterina Sedia, *Tangent* (reviewing "Krasnaya Luna")

"...instant classic..."
- *Sonic Society* (Referring to the radio play adaptation of Marlowe's short story "The Resident Member")

Table of Contents

Author's Foreword

SHORTLY AFTER THE commencement of hostilities in the last war with Germany, the Etheric Explorers Club deemed it advisable to vacate its premises on St Raphael's Square, London, due to the risk from aerial bombardment. Having in its possession a considerable store of documents and artefacts, the secretary of the club contacted The Body & Soul Society of Edinburgh with a view to securing a safe, temporary harbour for their archives. The then-president readily agreed to lend assistance to our sister-society, offering the accumulation of club papers a new home for the duration of the emergency at our own premises.

After some months, curiosity sent me delving into the documents to such an extent that I found myself devoting more and more of my time to their study. In particular, one class of papers caught my attention – those accounts of *outré* phenomena which were filed with the club's correspondence, but which were considered by the editors to be of too anecdotal a character, or insufficiently supported by evidence, to be published in their journal, *The Proceedings of the Etheric Explorers Club*. Thus, a large body of documentary matter existed which had received little attention, being gradually forgotten over the years. For my own amusement, I transformed a selection of the incidents into short stories, fleshing them out and giving them a more coherent form without taking undue liberties with the persons or events of the accounts. Where the actual names of participants are employed, permission to do so was obtained from those from whom the accounts originated, or their heirs; otherwise, names have been changed.

In 1947, the president returned the Etheric Explorers Club's archives to their repaired premises, but I begged leave to retain some of the anecdotal papers for further study. This request the club executive were gracious enough to grant, and it is out of the narratives developed therefrom that the current tales have been selected.

A few words about ether are, perhaps, necessary to clarify the subject. In the early 19th century, when anaesthetics were unknown, a fluid called "ether" was played with (one can hardly say "experimented with") at gatherings known as "ether frolics". At these get-togethers, friends would collect for a social evening of sniffing diethyl ether, also known as "sweet oil of vitriol". As can well be imagined, a roomful of merrymakers indulging in anaesthetic vapour led to no end of amusement, albeit amusement of a mildly sinister and parlous variety. The effects varied by individual. Some wept. Others were convulsed with laughter. Still others became truculent, and those who overindulged received total insensibility as their reward. This latter effect, combined with the observation that those who injured themselves during their antics rarely felt any pain (until they had returned to their senses), led to an understanding of the great potential of ether for relieving suffering during surgery. So, while diethyl ether is unconnected to the concept researched by the Etheric Explorers Club, there is nevertheless a parallel between the progressive understanding of the two substances: what began as amateur dabbling – "ether frolics" – culminated in a new science of the greatest utility to mankind.

It is worth noting that the etheric sciences researched by the club are also unrelated, at least directly, to the ether postulated in now-obsolete theories of light transmission, but deal with what Dr Raphael Maddox termed the *pneumatiferous ether*. Several versions of the pneumatiferous ether theory have had varying degrees of currency over the years since Dr Maddox proposed the concept, the dominant and most enduring being the proposition that our own cosmos is in fact the product of a merger or intersection between two once-separate universes, each bringing a distinct set of physical laws to the combined daughter cosmos that resulted – our own. One of the universes contributed the bulk of the matter and energy we observe today, while the other was what has been styled a "withered" or "failed" universe containing no matter, only the pneumatiferous ether, whose obscure effects account for many of what are commonly referred to as "supernatural" phenomena. Controversially, the theory has (according to some scholars), found confirmation in the so-called *Didyma Mechanism*, an extraordinarily intricate geared machine discovered at the turn of the century by divers near the Turkish coast, off-shore from the ancient city of Didyma, modern Didim. Embedded in a fused mass of pine resin – probably the result of fire aboard a ship carrying both the mechanism and a cargo of *Pinus halepensis* sap destined for the resination of wine – the device was in an almost perfect state of preservation, but suffered some damage during ill-conceived attempts to free it from the amber-like block that enclosed it. Given the dating evidence provided by other artefacts recovered from the wreck, the mechanism may have been a temple treasure of the local temple of Apollo – the Didymaion – that was placed aboard ship in an attempt to save it from the Gothic raids of the third century A.D. which were then causing panic in the region. (It has even been hypothesized that another copy of the mechanism existed at the Artemision in Ephesus, the destruction of which led the keepers of the Didyma copy to smuggle it from the city in order to preserve it from a similar fate.)

Several models of the mechanism, and the study of its inscriptions, seem to suggest that it was created as a kind of orrery to predict regular cycles of cosmological influence during which the effects of what was then believed to be magic were more or less pronounced according to the waxing and waning of the cycles. If true, this suggests an explanation for the seemingly fickle nature of "magical" or "spiritual" occurrences, as well as a means of predicting their decline during eras such as our own. Only further study will reveal whether the Didyma Mechanism is a will-o'-the-wisp or a new Rosetta Stone.

Finally, "Why a fox on the cover?" one might find oneself asking. If the reader will indulge a bit of wordplay on the part of the author, the explanation begins with the Japanese legends of the fox. Called *kitsune* in Japan, the fox was believed to have a natural affinity for magic, being capable of powerful illusions, including even the knowledge of how to transform into the likeness of any person. Sometimes friendly, sometimes mischievous, sometimes vengeful, *kitsune* are always emissaries from a world beyond the ordinary, and having nine tails is suggestive of a great and powerful *kitsune*. In this collection of stories we have nine *tales,* all stemming from that old, ambiguous institution, the Etheric Explorers Club, which has been by times a guardian, a source of wisdom, and even a stage for comedy or for tragedy; always a conduit for knowledge from those realms commonly called the supernatural. Visual puns of this variety have a venerable history in heraldry, in which field they are referred to as "canting". As the arms of The Body and Soul Society are of this type (having an escutcheon charged with a version of a mermaid, half Venus and half flatfish: bawdy & sole), it seems only appropriate to have these nine *tales* represented by nine *tails* when they are the tails of so sorcerous a beast as the *kitsune*.

Should the current collection of stories meet with interest from the public, I may delve deeper into the archives of the Etheric Explorers Club to provide further entertainment for the reader (and the author) through additional fictionalizations of records and anecdotes. It is the author's hope that readers may be sufficiently entertained by the tales that, as Baron Macaulay described the reception of Richard Quongti's *opus magnum* in his Lordship's "Prophetic Account of an Epic Poem"…*the sale will be so beneficial to the author that, instead of going about the dirty streets on his velocipede, he will be enabled to set up his balloon.*

Paul Marlowe
Honorary *Custos Rotolorum*
of the Etheric Explorers Club and
Fellow of The Body & Soul Society

Publisher's Note

It has not escaped the attention of the publisher that a discrepancy exists between, on the one hand, the apparent age of the author, Mr Marlowe (who, while not in the full bloom of youth, is obviously a relatively young man), and on the other the fact that he describes his participation in events of the 1940s – a period now over seventy years ago. It is the position of this publishing house that such statements arise from a literary conceit, or device (we decline to speculate as to the exact nature of the device). Consequently, the publisher asks that the public kindly direct any queries relating to the matter *to the author, not the publisher.*

Part I

WE BEGIN, IN a sense, at the end. The Etheric Explorers Club
was born in the midst of the so-called *Pax Britannica*, when
progress was gradually coming to seem like the natural order of
things. Reform proceeded at a pace which was too slow for some,
too rapid for others, but which did nonetheless advance without
unravelling the society that sustained that progress. It was a time in
which conscientious individuals strove to end the shameful practices of slavery and child labour, and for a while it seemed that
even war might be contained or prevented. Suffrage expanded, and
colonies grew towards independence. Laws and conscience began
to rein in industry, while reason defeated disease. Even the greatest mysteries seemed within the grasp of man. With the Great War
came the end of many things, not least among them the certainty
that the past held works and customs as valuable as present fash-
ions, and that civilization was improving in a myriad ways worth
striving for; worth dying for if need be — worth devoting one's
life to, preferably. Those who see only the failures of their pre-
decessors — or who merely mine the past in search of rhetorical
coals to heap on the fires of present-day grievances — may think
this a sentimental view of the Victorian era, and of history. James
Hilton's reply is the best, made when he reflected upon the close
of that epoch: "I do not object to being called a sentimentalist because I acknowledge the passing of a great age with something
warmer than a sneer."

Conceived as a place for individuals with common interests
in the etheric sciences to share the results of their research, the
Etheric Explorers Club was destined to take a more practical, collective interest in preserving the common good when there arose,
late in the 19th century, a series of crises which called for their spe-
cialized knowledge (crises too serious and too complex to delve

into in the present volume). In this way, the etheric sciences followed the pattern of so many other branches of knowledge, starting in abstract curiosity, and subsequently playing a part in affairs of state. So it was with the physics of motion being applied to cannon-shot trajectories, and chemistry to the powder; steam was first a toy, then a tool for draining mines, and eventually it came to power the engines of dreadnoughts. Inevitably the Great War changed the club, for in total war all of the resources of the warring nations are drawn into the conflict. For the first time, aerial bombardment by airship and aeroplane was employed, together with submarines, poison gas, tanks, and countless other technologies. And in their desperation to break out of the catastrophic stalemate of trench warfare, even stranger weapons were devised, and strange countermeasures used. It is fitting that in this disastrous rift between, on the one hand, the Victorian age together with its Edwardian afterglow, and on the other the twentieth century of fascism, communism, revolution, mass communication, fleeting fads, international corporations, and continual warfare, there should be a new generation taking up the torch; in the case of the first two tales, the grandchildren of club founder Rafe Maddox. Both Melissa and George Maddox were intimately involved in what might be called the hidden or occult war, waged in parallel with the war of artillery, bayonets, and Zeppelins.

In connexion with the painting described in "Ten Golden Roosters", it is worth noting that the work is (along with Melissa Maddox's 1914 expense claim for 200 francs, and the artist's own absinthe spoon) on display at the club, where it can be viewed on visiting days upon payment of the very reasonable fee of one shilling, or a thruppenny bit for children. The head of the knight Roland, artistically wrought in the medieval style, may also be viewed, along with Dr Rafe Maddox's pneumatypograph apparatus, books of spirit-communication transcripts, and a great number of other interesting and illuminating exhibits. Melissa Maddox herself preferred not to draw any definite conclusions as to whether Vasily Rubinoff's art demonstrated signs of what is sometimes referred to as "the intuitive apprehension of multiple etheric probabilities". She did say, however, say that it was a disturbing addition to the age-old debate on the question of free will versus predestination.

In response to my several queries in regards to the permissibility of publishing a fictional account of the events described in "The Last Post", the War Office has replied by assuring me that there is not, nor has there ever been, a section of the Directorate of Military Intelligence named M.I.10 (e). Therefore, I have concluded that there can be no possible objection to describing the activities of an agency which has never existed. George Maddox who — if anyone — should know, commented in his approval of my publication of this tale that this response was "typical Janusine bureaucratic balderdash, damn their eyes," and went on to make a number of other comments which I judged, on the whole, better left unprinted. (Apparently, by 'Janusine', Maddox was alluding to the two-faced nature of the god Janus, though I can find no record of this word being used by any person aside from Maddox).

Readers may notice that in the story "The Penitent of Grinsfield" the narrative perspective is, unlike in the other eight tales, in the third person. It is not a mere accident that this is the case, for the original account itself arrived third hand, in contrast to those which were the foundation of other stories in this collection. "Father Drewitt" (whose name and parish were changed) did not record the events himself, for reasons which will be obvious.

It is sad to relate that Drewitt died at Monte Cassino during the Italian Campaign of the Second World War. Given his condition at the end — delirium — his story would be easy to discard as the product of a feverish mind near death; readers are left to draw their own conclusions. What is know is that Drewitt's tale was heard by a military doctor who, because of his native cynicism, was inclined to regard Drewitt's "ramblings" as something of a joke, at least in part because Drewitt had believed the physician to be another priest. It happened that George Maddox (again in the service of the non-existent M.I. 10 (e)) was a subsequent patient of this same doctor, and it was Maddox who ultimately submitted the account to the club. Even *in extremis*, it appears that Drewitt never revealed the details of the confession which lies at the heart of his tale, only the penitent's identity.

Ten Golden Roosters

GRANDFATHER MADDOX HAD made arrangements to interview an artist at a particular café in Paris, but when the opportunity subsequently arose for him to meet with the new director of the Kaiser Wilhelm Physical Institute in Berlin, he was forced to choose between the two appointments, sending me in his stead to France. It was with some reluctance that I accepted, for although it was an attractive prospect to spend that splendid June in Paris, I was not altogether content to be seeking the company of a mad Russian, no matter how talented he was reputed to be. Had that been my desire, I could have satisfied it more quickly by attending Diaghilev's *Ballets Russes*, which was performing *Le Coq d'Or* at the hideously garish Paris Opera.

By the time four tedious days had passed, I had cultivated an intense dislike of the Café Warsaw, with its tin Pernod signs, its greasy zinc counters, and its cheap furniture lacquered in filth. Even the lurid newspaper stories that I was forced to occupy myself with, of the *Empress of Ireland* tragedy and other affairs, were growing tiresome. It was only mid-afternoon, but already the café was full of merry-making Parisians smoking coarse tobacco or taking other stimulants. On my left a trio of young women of about my own age, eighteen or nineteen perhaps, dressed apparently for the stage of *Les Folies Bergère*, were taking turns animatedly relating segments of a rather risqué anecdote, accompanied by wails of laughter. A funk of turpentine hung in the air, emanating from the artistic clientèle perhaps, or from the liquor. Moreover I was growing unhappy with Vasily Rubinoff, who seemed disinclined to make his appearance at the arranged location.

While I felt a certain pity for many of the more bedraggled customers, the constant importuning of a succession of slovenly men was leaving me with an even more unfavourable impression of the city's morals than that with which I had arrived. As another middle-aged specimen manoeuvred toward me, I hastily endeavoured to construct some suitably brusque French rebuke, but he merely examined me briefly and smiled, took an adjoining table, and ordered coffee and a meal.

From his familiar manner, the man appeared to frequent the café, and he had an intelligently respectable face. I decided to inquire as to whether he was acquainted with Rubinoff. Withdrawing a photograph of the painter, I approached the man.

"*Excusez-moi monsieur. Je crois que vous mangez ici régulièrement et je me demandais si vous connaissez cet homme, Vasily Rubinoff?*"

"*La Vache? Mais oui.* But you're English, aren't you miss?"

"Why yes, I am. And you are an American?"

"Well, I prefer the term *North* American. Canadian actually. Robert Service."

"Pleased to meet you, Mr Service. I am Melissa Maddox. This man, *La Vache* did you call him? Why 'The Cow'?"

"Oh, you see 'Vasha' is short for Vasily, and it's just gotten transmuted into 'Vache'. I suppose it was on account of his mooing monotone. That, and he loves to graze on the green fog. Or rather, is compelled to from some hunger. I can't say as I've ever seen a sign that *La Vache* loves anything."

"The green fog?"

"Absinthe, Miss Maddox. You'll want to return in a few hours for *l'heure verte*, when the devotees of the green goddess come for libations. That's generally when *La Vache* takes his breakfast."

One of the young women from the next table overheard us and exclaimed her assistance.

"Ho! You look for *La Vache, hein*? His studio is close by. Do you like to go there?"

"Thank-you, miss?"

"Jeanette!"

"Thank-you, but I will look for him here this evening, rather than wake him."

She made some Gallic sign of resignation and returned to her friends' laughter. Mr Service waved at an empty chair in invitation, and not wishing to be ungrateful, I joined him. Despite his attire, he seemed a gentleman, and was wearing a wedding band, which was the more reassuring once I understood that he was not French.

"I thought that absinthe was banned, Mr Service. Does this man Rubinoff drink to excess?"

"Some more timid nations have outlawed it, but the French are valiant in their pleasures, Miss Maddox. As for *La Vache*, he drinks a great deal, and having seen the results of sobriety in him, I daresay I approve of his drunkenness. But what brings you to see him? Surely you're not a relative? Or would you buy some of his paintings, maybe?"

"His art *is* the purpose of my visit."

"I'd say you have an adventurous spirit, Miss Maddox, in art at any rate."

"I suppose he is very *avant garde*?"

"You know him only by reputation, then?"

"Hardly even that. My grandfather has an interest in Rubinoff, but was unable to keep his appointment here. He wishes to have my impressions of the man and of his work so as to report on them to his club. He believes Rubinoff may be of some interest to them."

"Your grandfather is an art *aficionado*, then?"

"I am afraid he did not share his reasoning with me before his departure. However, I am assuming his interest is of a more scientific nature. Grandfather has a theory concerning the nature of consciousness, in which the mind is both an organ and a manifestation of the ether. One is matter, while the other is spirit. He has spent a considerable part of his life perfecting the apparatus to probe the etheric component of the mind, and presumably he wishes to investigate the particular etheric signature of the artistic mind. This is merely a surmise on my part, however. Grandfather is a trifle terse in his communications at times."

Mr Service considered this for a moment.

"Vache's work is… unusual. Rather obsessed with war and decay. Maybe it's because he's Russian."

"Have you seen many of his paintings?"

"A few. I can't say that I seek them out. In some ways they remind me of Bruegel, the Elder, that is. Dark things, full of curiously ugly people. Not so many Dutchmen and devils as Bruegel, though. Once, I recall, he carried about a triptych that folded up into a box. The first panel showed the face of a rather dull but dissolute young man on a Paris street. The next, the same man, hollow-cheeked now and hopeless, drably outfitted, in a ditch of some kind, up to his knees in water and clouded in smoke. The third, a rotting skull in the mud with a bootprint across it."

"He has not been a great commercial success, then."

"Not that I've seen any signs of."

Eager to escape the café, if only for an hour or two, I bade Mr Service *adieu*, and made a quick trip to a *Bureau de Poste et Télégraphie* to send a telegramme to Grandfather.

SIR RAFE MADDOX
EIDOLON GESELLSCHAFT
WILHELMSTRASSE BERLIN
ALLEMAGNE

RUBINOFF ABSINTHE MAD DRUNKARD IS INTER-
VIEW STILL NECESSARY MELISSA

I could not imagine what Grandfather's interest was in Rubinoff's morbid paintings, and would rather have avoided the meeting from what I had heard of the man. Unfortunately, near five p.m., a reply arrived at my hotel saying simply 'YES'.

Forced to return to the odious café, I was no sooner in the door than I beheld Rubinoff in a *fracas* with the waiter over the price of meals, and the unavailability of credit. Approaching them, I was surprised at what a pale, depressing little man Rubinoff was in person, waving large and grubby hands as his unshaven face droned at the unfortunate waiter. When I sought the painter's attention, however, he curtly shooed me away in accented French.

"Go away woman. I can afford no *putain* tonight," he told me.

I could not conceive why he imagined me to be a pudding-seller, but was obligated to disabuse him of the notion nonetheless.

"Sir, I am Melissa Maddox, here on behalf of Dr Rafe Maddox, with whom you made an appointment."

Rubinoff had a look of momentary confusion, which the waiter took advantage of by making a rude gesture, quickly departing to serve another customer. I motioned to indicate that we might take a table. Rubinoff slouched into a chair, though his dull, confused expression suggested that he was not sure why.

"We will have absinthe," he stated, rather perfunctorily, I thought.

"You may, sir, if you have any money, which I doubt, but I will not be joining you. I am here to learn about your work, not to poison myself."

Rubinoff regarded me witheringly for a moment before laughing uproariously and smacking the table with one hand.

"*Da*, I have a few *sous* left. Waiter!"

When he had ordered his drink, he nodded ponderously. As quickly as his mirth had risen he now drooped, as if someone had turned the gaslights suddenly up and down.

"Maddox, I remember him. Came through here with a Kodak, talking about a lot of nonsenses. What is he wanting now?"

"He is interested in your paintings, and would have me assess them, as he was unable to be here himself."

"Painting is an agony. Let us not speak of it tonight."

He drew a curiously slotted spoon out of his coat pocket when his small glass of absinthe arrived, accompanied by a lump of sugar and a pitcher of water, which were set upon the table once the waiter had counted Rubinoff's coins. The painter arranged the things before him and produced a box of matches, evidently readying himself to prepare the drink.

"If you do not wish to discuss your work, then there is no point in my remaining. I will leave you to your unsavoury ritual."

As I was about to depart, Rubinoff arrested me with a comment which was so peculiar that I remained seated.

"Ritual is a song that sings the mind to sleep," he told me, in the midst of his preparations.

"What do you mean by that?"

He did not reply immediately, but ignited the liquor-soaked sugar on his spoon, and then mixed the melting syrup into the absinthe, finally adding water until the glass swirled with greenish opalescence, releasing the resinous liquorice-scent that I had noticed earlier, during my vigil.

"Ritual, Miss Maddox. The *Marseillaise* that the *poilus* sing as they march into the machine guns. The last rites as we die. They send reason to sleep so it will not recoil from the horror of extinction, so we will not scream all the way to the grave."

Perhaps the man was mad, or in love with death, but he was evidently not the shallow wastrel that I had originally taken him for.

"Is that why you take absinthe, to silence your mind?"

He sipped the foul liquid with a grimace of gloomy satisfaction.

"I have good eyes, I think. I can see a long way, longer than I like. Absinthe is like twilight. The world goes dark. I see just me, and you, and that dog of a waiter, and all these other poor fools who come in from the night and go back to it. And no-one cares what becomes of them."

"You feel compassion for these unfortunates then?"

"Call it compassion. They are miserable. I am miserable. We are stuck where we are."

As Rubinoff was ordering more of the cheap liquor with his last pieces of change, I took the opportunity to ask the waiter for something to eat, if only to conduct the conversation along lines of semi-sobriety. Plates soon arrived with bread, butter, cold roast chicken, and *café au lait*, as well as the absinthe, which was temporarily set aside while Rubinoff gorged on the food.

"You sound as though you may be a socialist, Mr Rubinoff. Is that what brought you to Paris? Or was it art?"

Wiping his lips with the back of his hand, he cast an unfocused stare out the window and through the passers-by.

"Russia. I did not like to leave. But it pained me to stay there. I saw bad times ahead for the *Rodina* – for Mother Russia. Very bad." He returned to eating, but paused, as an afterthought. "I belong to no parties. I abominate parties."

This statement he fairly spat out. Politics was clearly something he felt some passion for. "I do hope you are not an anarchist," I said, half-convinced that he probably was.

"All government is corrupt. Palaces of pigs who lord over men. Oh, here in France they may choose new pigs every few years. In Russia we get the first boar to come out of the Tsar's sow. Is no different. They are all swine."

I nodded, sipping my coffee. He *was* an anarchist, then.

"Many Russians," he continued, "believe anarchism will bring them utopia. They plot, they make bombs, some go to Siberia. It means nothing. We have instincts to be tyrants and slaves. There will always be another Tsar, another president, another capitalist. We could kill, and kill, and one of us would just put on the crown in the end, or the top hat."

"It seems a very pessimistic philosophy. Why do you paint then? Why do anything?"

He shrugged. "It is desire I have. Hopeless men have few desires. I indulge mine. It is foolish, but I do it."

"Surely painting is not foolish, if done well at any rate."

"Pointless to create things. They will just be destroyed by fools. Look at the Tuileries. The greatest palace in Paris once. Emperors lived there. Kings. Built over generations. Burnt one night by a mob of Communards. Now is utterly gone. In a little while, no-one will even remember. We are in our own beautiful palace, of glass. One man with a stone will bring it all down on our heads."

He was avoiding my gaze, toying idly with the remains of the chicken on his plate, though with eyes occasionally straying to the untouched absinthe. Finally he succumbed to the temptation, and began clearing away the scraps of food to make room for his drinking ritual.

"The food is terrible in this country. There is no place to get good *baursaki* like at home," he said.

"I am not familiar with the dish."

"It is," he began, apparently lacking the words to describe its delectability. He defined a vague, indeterminate shape with his big limp hands. "It is a fried thing. Eaten with soup. Very good."

Not sure whether this meant an oyster or a pancake, I nodded again, which seemed the only acknowledgement he required.

"French make good absinthe, though. Only thing that keeps me sane. You have absinthe in England?"

"In England it is generally considered injurious to one's health. The distinctive ingredient, wormwood, is poisonous."

Before him, the loathsome drinking paraphernalia were all arranged, and Rubinoff dipped his sugar spoon into the liquor. Lighting it with a match, he sat mesmerised by the blue and orange light, inhaling the cloying vapours.

"Anise. Fennel. Wormwood. Mugwort." Rubinoff looked up from his glass. "Mugwort. In Russia we call it *polyn*, or *chernobyl*."

Once or twice, as he held the flaming spoon, he repeated the word. Incredibly, he grew even paler. A palsy seemed to grip him suddenly, and the spoon fell from his trembling hand into the glass, igniting the rest of the liquor. He sprang to his feet and away from the table, eyes still fixed on the glass.

"Chernobyl," he rasped, "burning."

He stumbled clumsily out through the café door like a drunken man, but with a rigid mask of terror on his face.

Rubinoff had left me at a loss for something to do, since it hardly felt seemly for me to go chasing through Montparnasse after the raving little man. Unsure of how to proceed, I sat watching the flickering blue flame flowing to and fro in the glass. Was the matter worth pursuing any further, or was the painter only a lunatic after all?

Just then, Mr Service appeared, to my surprise.

"I hope you'll forgive me, Miss Maddox, but I was interested in how your interview with *La Vache* would go. Evidently not well, as it turned out."

"Please, sit if you like."

He did, after first placing a saucer over the absinthe glass to extinguish it.

"You must have offered some rather frank criticism of his work to send him off like that," he told me, I think jokingly.

"Not at all; in fact we were simply discussing food and drink, when he seemed to take a rather violent dislike to the absinthe."

"Odd. Then again, he's always peculiar, so what can you expect? A lot of these artist chaps are odd fish."

We chatted away amiably for some time about the many unusual characters that Mr Service had met in Paris, frequently interrupted by the bumps of passing inebriates, and once by a rather loud report from a passing motor car. Much of Mr Service's time is spent composing a queer sort of doggerel, as it turns out, which he apparently finds highly amusing. He went on to quote considerable passages of it while we drank the bottle of wine that he purchased. Yet all the while, I was feeling that I did not like to leave Grandfather's errand incomplete. Eventually we came back to the subject.

"Do you suppose that I might visit Mr Rubinoff's studio, to view his art? I would like to have something more to report to my grandfather than that I briefly discussed politics and fried foods before frightening Rubinoff away."

"Well, you might if either of us knew the way," he suggested, rather unhelpfully. Then he thought for a moment, and snapped his fingers.

"That girl, what was her name? The one who offered to take you earlier. I think I saw her tonight."

By now it was growing more difficult to hear ourselves amid the din in the crowded café. Mr Service stood up to peer through the smoky haze hovering above the heads of the patrons, and almost at once he pointed to someone, whom he went to question.

When they returned in a few moments, I could see by the way she was grinning and leaning languorously on Mr Service that Jeannette had been imbibing more than just the one glass of absinthe that was in her hand.

"Jeannette, would you mind taking us to Monsieur Rubinoff's studio to view his work?"

She lurched forward and patted my lapels in a rather familiar manner.

"*Bien sûr!* He lives in my *bâtiment*, not far away. *À votre santé!*"

Jeannette gulped down the rest of her absinthe, and we followed her out onto street. As we progressed towards her boarding house, it became increasingly obvious that there was some stir or excitement in the neighbourhood, although the cause was not immediately apparent. With occasional support from one or both of us, Jeannette steered us along the distance of a couple of blocks. But as we turned the final corner, we saw a multitude gathered on the pavement beside the building, large enough that people were spilling out onto the street and obstructing traffic. In the midst of it, a small group of firemen were coiling their hoses and returning them to the engine. Jeannette was insistent upon getting to the front of the crowd, and so we edged forward across the wet cobbles towards the reek of scorched wood emanating from a smashed window on the first floor.

Arriving close to the centre of the activity, Jeannette began interrogating an on-looker, who was evidently another of her neighbours. From snatches of the conversation, we learnt that sometime earlier there had been a gas explosion, followed by a fire which had consumed one flat before it was subdued by the fire brigade. The blast must have been the source of the noise that Mr Service and I had taken for a back-firing motor as we talked in the café.

"*Oh, non!*" we heard Jeannette exclaim, though we did not know why until we peered over her shoulder, to where Rubinoff's charred body was resting on a stretcher, beside a *gendarme* who was probably awaiting a conveyance for the corpse. I touched Jeannette's arm sympathetically, and she threw herself upon me, weeping. I did what I could to comfort her, and eventually Mr Service suggested that we return her to her apartment, as the residents were now being allowed back into the building.

Inside, we sat Jeannette down and poured her a little brandy to calm her.

"Poor Vache, it's too terrible," she said.

"An awful accident," Mr Service agreed, though sounding doubtful. He cast a glance at me.

Seeing this, Jeannette sniffed and shook her head. "*Non*. I think he did it. Poor Vache. He must have put out the pilot lights. Such a sad man. But a good man. Once, when I had nothing to eat, he gave me thirty francs, and he wanted nothing in return."

We stayed briefly to see that her nerves had settled, but Jeannette was remarkably resilient, and we soon were readying ourselves to leave her to her private thoughts.

"I suppose I shall never have the opportunity now to view his paintings. No doubt they were all consumed in the blaze that followed the explosion," I said.

"Paintings? But I have one. He gave it to me," Jeannette replied, leading us to the wall where it lay, shrouded in a sheet of canvas. "You see," she said, unwrapping it to show us. "I could not decide to hang it or not. It is… a difficult thing to see."

It was. Intricate and monstrous, it was all that was left of Rubinoff's strange talent. I was struck by an impulse to possess it, if only to have something to show for an otherwise wasted journey.

"I know it must have sentimental value for you Jeannette, but would you consider selling it to me? Perhaps for say, two hundred francs?"

She glanced at the canvas, but cast down her eyes as a little *frisson* seemed to go through her.

"Yes," she agreed.

I counted out ten gold *Napoléons*, or rather *coqs d'or*, for of course the Emperor was long gone now, replaced by a golden rooster. She took the coins.

"Poor Vache," she said again as we parted at the door, "Do you think he saw his own end as well?"

"What do you mean, saw it?"

"*Presentiments*, or *reveries* of the future. They tormented his sleep, and even in the day. *Mon Dieu*, at least he has some peace now."

Back on the street, I waved my parasol to hail one of the taximeter cabs that were passing by. One rattled up to the curb and the driver held the door while I stowed away my painting and climbed aboard.

"I appreciate all of your assistance, Mr Service. Here is my card, if you ever find yourself in London," I told him though the cab window.

"It was no trouble, Miss Maddox. Do you believe any of that talk of second sight? Was that what interested your grandfather, do you suppose?"

"I really do not know what to make of it, though it is the sort of matter he is inclined to investigate. Perhaps he will explain when I see him next. It was a pleasure to make your acquaintance."

We shook hands though the window, and I told the cabman to depart. On the journey towards the Seine I reflected upon the day's strange events, and grew more convinced that Grandfather had indeed been curious about Rubinoff's reputation for precognition, and had wished to see samples of the visions portrayed in Rubinoff's art. At least I had been able to bring him a specimen, if a disturbing one. One could only hope that the scene portrayed there bore no relation to anything that might await mankind.

Driving over the arches of the *pont Royal* towards the *Pavil-*

lion de Flore, with its tall chimneys and steep trapezoidal mansard roof, I realised that we would soon pass the site of the old Tuileries Palace. As it was yet not very late, and I felt too restless to return immediately to my hotel, I asked the driver to deliver me to the park opposite the *Pavillion*.

After the long hours of confinement in the stuffy Café Warsaw, it was a relief to have the chance to use my legs on the broad avenues of what was now just the Tuileries Gardens. Despite the somewhat rigid and classical formality of the place, it was peaceful and fresh. For an hour, or perhaps more, I strolled amongst the trees and pools, which seemed nearly deserted compared with the bustle of Montparnasse. A few old men, perhaps veterans of the campaigns of the last Napoléon, sat enjoying the cool night air, while couples wandered together in quiet conversation.

In time the canvas I had purchased, which was slightly longer than my arm, grew to be a wearisome burden. I found myself a bench by a fountain where my benumbed fingers could recover awhile. There was enough lamplight to see by, and so I uncovered the painting to examine it once again.

As Mr Service had said, it was indeed much like Bruegel's *Triumph of Death*, only the emaciated skeletal wretches in this image appeared to be not the servants of death, but the pathetic survivors of the living. In a barren landscape of ruins and burnt shells of buildings, faceless men with black uniforms herded the skeletons before bayonets into pits, where they seemed to reach thin arms at the viewer, while their fellows buried them alive. The executioners bore unfamiliar, almost magical icons, such as stars, runes, and fylfots or *crux gammata*. Everywhere the black-clad soldiers were attending gibbets, burning books, or brooding over hills of skulls, and in the muddy sky flocks of black aeroplanes dropped fire onto ruined cities.

I wrapped the painting once more. Perhaps there was something in Rubinoff's judgement of great works like the Tuileries Palace. Destruction is so simple, while building can be the work of lifetimes. Nations have long memories of their pains and grudges. It is sometimes what holds them together, and what keeps them at the throats of their neighbours. But as Rubinoff said, though, people forget. Most in the Tuileries that night had probably forgotten the burnt palace and thought only of the blooms and the trees, or of their companions, which is just as well.

The Last Post

A HAGGARD-LOOKING MESSENGER ARRIVED in the morning at my office (such as it was — a ruined cottage near the Italian lines north of Venice) as I was blotting the report on my latest activities. My plan had been to celebrate by installing two feet on a wobbly three-legged stool so as to enjoy a refreshing Aspirin bottle-full of well deserved *grappa* in the proper attitude of relaxation; the previous resident of the house had taken his liqueur glasses with him when he fled the war zone, if he ever had any, and I'd gone though my limited supply of analgesics.

It has been a busy fortnight, involving the delicate infiltration of a Dalmatian into the Austro-Hungarian forces that were in control of a line from the mountains to the Adriatic.

A Dalmatian *nurse*, not a dog.

Apart from her devotion to independence for the Kingdom of Dalmatia, she possessed an exceptional ability not only to dream lucidly, but also to project her dreams into the sleeping minds of others. It was an operation which succeeded admirably, so much so that I had planned a spot of holidaying as a reward, to whit, popping down to Ravenna to see the city where the celebrated Gothic warlord Theodoric had seized the crown of Italy by cleaving the previous king, Odoacer, in two. I understood that Theodoric's Mausoleum was worth a look, and the prospect of a hot bath, clean sheets, and cooked meals was even more inviting.

"There is no peace, saith the Lord, unto the wicked," I told the courier, accepting the despatch box from him and cracking its seals. No harm in seeing what it was. I waved a hospitable hand towards the Aspirin bottle, which he drained gratefully in a gulp.

Surprisingly, it wasn't typical of the communiques that followed a dazzlingly successful mission, such as "Priorities changed: undo everything". Rather, another potential assignment. Not the most attractive, perhaps, as its purpose was to determine the nature of, and possible countermeasures to, an enemy weapon of unknown nature. Reading on through the briefing papers, I learned that the weapon was unknown because it had killed everyone who had had the misfortune to encounter it. In a rather nasty way, in fact. Or, to be scrupulous, everyone but for a lone survivor who had merely been driven mad. As the last two attacks had fallen upon prominent salients on the Western Front, carried out at the time of the dark moon, the weapon was expected to be employed again … I checked my watch … tonight. Something about the weapon's *modus occidendi* seemed too ironic to pass up, given the holiday plans I'd been formulating. I admit, too, that it intrigued me simply because I couldn't think what the weapon might be.

"You came by air," I assumed. "When can we leave?"

The messenger coughed. "My engine died outside Verona. It will take a few days to get spares."

"Not good enough, I'm afraid."

I swept the report into my satchel along with the despatch case, the *grappa* bottle, and my other odds and ends, leaving my guest to enjoy the limited attractions of my erstwhile H.Q. while I set out for the nearest aerodrome of the *Corpo Aeronautico Militare*. The commander, when I arrived, wasn't aloft himself, so I posed my problem to him without any preliminaries. "It is essential that I reach the front in France by tonight, *Maggiore*, and the *Corpo Aeronautico* are the most skilled mountain flyers in the world. Can you get me over the Alps and into France in time?" He assured me (no doubt influenced by my letter of introduction from General Diaz) that the C.A.M. would be pleased to assist me in any way, including an unscheduled flight to France. I thanked him, perhaps a little floridly, and telegraphed to my contact in London: *ALBION ACCEPTS.*

Flattery aside, the pilot he assigned to me — Bellini — was a fine flyer. Hour upon hour of an open observer's cockpit does tend to wear a fellow out, however, even with the best pilot, particularly when the engine keeps backfiring with bursts of flame. At least the sun blazed away in the clear skies over Lombardy, without warmth at that height. We paused at the FIAT 'drome outside Turin, where I filled a pair of Thermoses with strong, hot coffee, and posted a card of the *Palazzo* to Amanda during the fuelling of Bellini's recce plane. I would have sent one to my sister, Melissa, as well, but God only knew where she was at any given moment. The next hop took us over the Alps, and if flying backwards across the Veneto, Lombardy, and Piedmont had been tiring, watching the peaks of the Alps loom out of clouds and drift past my ears within range of the rear-pointing observer's machine gun was as chilling as the air at that altitude. But then, I never like travelling with my back to the engine. More chilling even than the 125 mph draught blowing down my collar was the mulling-over I did in the air, of the background matter of my assignment. Another new enemy weapon, naturally; that's all my section handled. New, *non-standard* weapons. They'd been kind enough to include photographs of the aftermath of Death's sickle in this particular instance. An entire company had been minced where it stood. My task was to photograph the next mincing in progress, to find out what was responsible, so that countermeasures could be developed.

Beyond the Alps and Switzerland, we flew parallel to the lines in France, the scale of the front apparent in a way it never was from ground level. Brown scars zigzagged in a vast wound across the world, stretching from horizon to horizon, where the continent was tearing itself apart; a crack to Hell opening in Europe's skin, one that millions of men had rushed to close up with their bodies. How *many* millions of bodies would it need to close up a wound like that? Or would it ever heal? Bellini, in the cockpit, his back to mine, tapped my shoulder, shaking me out of apocalyptic reveries. There was a Royal Bavarian *Jagdstaffel*, my map said, just across the lines. I limbered up my fingers and fired a few rounds from the rear gun to warm it up, in case the Jasta across the way had any of their scouts aloft today, to pick off daydreaming aviators. The Italian sight-seeing tour was over.

We were lucky, and the German flyers found better objects for their attention that day. By the time we bumped down at the aerodrome in France I felt as if I'd spent a day passing though a gelato factory, alternately shaken, stirred, and frozen. I stretched and stamped on the tarmac to get some feeling back into my limbs. When I could move again, I shook Bellini's hand.

"*Grazie*, Bellini," I said, checking my wristwatch. "I've got to be moving along. Safe return to you."

"*Addio*, Maddox. She's not so bad, the 7b," he said, patting the wing. "Sometimes, her wings fall off, but not today."

Decent chap, I thought, for waiting until we'd landed to tell me that.

I have nothing against aviation. Half an hour in the air is as exhilarating an experience as anything you can mention, and some things you can't. A fine achievement, dreamt of for countless generations since Icarus, now achieved at last. And since that air journey from Verona to France, in the back of a dodgy two seater, an achievement which will continue haunting dreams - mine, at any rate. Though no more than what happened in the trenches afterwards.

After cadging a lift to a nearby stores depot where M.I. had stashed my equipment, I cadged another to the front, in the back of a truck delivering munitions. All in all, I think Bellini's plane gave a more comfortable ride than the the solid-tyred lorry laden with several tons of rattling high explosives. The crates — stencilled "Yospher Munitions Company" — at least made a rough and ready *escritoire* on which to balance the dregs of one of the Thermoses, and lay out the background papers on the matter at hand, which hadn't been convenient to read in an open cockpit. Not that there was much to work with. A raving account from a shell-shock case, some ghastly photographs, and figures of the casualties. The nails embedded in some of the dead were a puzzling point of interest, one which demonstrated the thoroughness of Intelligence: after exhaustive research, they had been enabled to conclude without the slightest uncertainty that the nails were *definitely* German nails. Even if Military Intelligence had made a Herculean effort to spin the paltry evidence into a more official-sounding thread, there are only so many ways to say "We know little or nothing, because everyone died". When I found myself browsing the camera training manual even though I was familiar with most photographic equipment (it was a camera, tripod, and associated paraphernalia that M.I. had left at the depot), I decided there was nothing more to be gleaned from the reports. The truth would out eventually — more's the pity.

We kept jouncing over what passed for road, with what passed for ambulances creeping by the opposite way, shaking what life was left out of their cargo. From the breast pocket of my Mac I prised out a wad of Amanda's letters to pass the time until we reached the Front, more coffee being contraindicated after a jolt sent the remains of Thermos № 1 splashing over my dossier of intelligence. The letters weren't quite up to the minute on recent events, having drifted in *poste restante* over weeks at British consulates in my general neighbourhood, but they were better than life at present.

> *... father will no longer tolerate having your name mentioned in his presence, while mother sends her regards in the shape of the enclosed white feathers. Perhaps if you had been a Quaker, they might have understood. Not approved of, but understood. To refuse to accept conscription because you find it tyrannical to have a puffed-up functionary of the government wield power over you — the power to order you to dress as he commands, march as he commands, go where and do what he commands, and kill whom he commands — is a stand which I whole-heartedly support, dearest, believe me. Mother and Father, I am afraid, are more in sympathy with the Board which consigned you to a cell. You are quite right that killing is sometimes justified, while allowing another to order you to kill is never morally correct ...*

When the lorry lurched across a shallow crater, I edged away from the rickety tail-gate in case it gave way and dropped me under the wheels of the following lorry. That interview with the Board judging conshie cases had been a less-than-chummy one. They often encountered subjects of His Majesty whose consciences refused to countenance killing, and so the Board were consequently used to bullying their charges into accepting some form of non-combat slavery; what they had trouble with was one who objected to authority more than to murder — murder in a good cause, of course. I waxed quite eloquent when telling them I'd give my last drop of blood for my country ... refusing all the while to give a

damn what anyone ordered me to do. Arguments about the poison-
ing of British liberty with Prussian militarism failed to move them,
and in the end the Board recommended an indefinite period in one
of His Majesty's prisons as the best way for me to serve my country in wartime, as an example to other would-be non-conformists.
Amanda went on,

> ... *I must say, they were high-minded men, those*
> *guards, ready and willing to sacrifice their chance*
> *to die in the trenches, all for the sake of doing*
> *their patriotic duty of helping improve any of their*
> *countrymen who suffered from an excess of con-*
> *science, using those old instruments of charity, the*
> *hobnailed boot, the fist, and the filth on the dinner*
> *tray ...*

Oh, yes, we had a high old time indeed at the Richmond Castle
prison.

Though where Amanda acquired such a bitter turn of phrase
was a mystery. Probably in the suffrage movement. The author-
ities had been known for their gentle methods in that emergency
as well.

A few weeks into my enjoyment of official hospitality, my cell
received a visit from a gentleman, Sir Odbur Sikes, to whom I offered my plank as the best available seating. He looked like one of
those heavily-lined marble busts of dyspeptic Roman republican
patricians. I stood, looking no doubt like a well-beaten egg in my
broad-arrow prison suit.

"The facilities are a trifle primitive," I told him apologetically
(and a little thickly, as my lip hadn't yet healed). "Shall we ring the
guard for tea? Seeing as how you're a man of some distinction, he
probably won't spit in it."

"Cynicism is not attractive, Mr Maddox."

"Neither is imprisonment, Sir Odbur."

"Yes, well, you have only yourself to blame for that. I was
visiting your grandfather at his house in Kent. We spoke of you."

"How is old Sir Rafe? It must have been like a *weekend* for the
pair of you: two knights away from work."

"Very droll, Mr Maddox. Do you wish to know why I have

come?"

"If it is because you share my conviction, Sir Odbur, I'm obliged to inform you that I won't willingly share my *plank* come bedtime, not without a fight."

Sir O kept up the same bland mask he'd worn since arriving, as if to say he was impervious to any number of assaults by idiocy. I shrugged, and gestured for him to have his say.

"I am aware, Mr Maddox, that you have assisted your grandfather in a number of his interests. He speaks highly of your resourcefulness, if not your tractability. As you object so strenuously to military discipline, I am here to offer you an opportunity to contribute usefully to the nation's defence in a different capacity."

I stroked the stubble on my chin. It really was disgraceful, the way my standards had been sinking lately. "More useful than my current role, as a punching-bag for Officer Verges?" (Not his real moniker, merely my little pet name for him).

"I am proposing that you join Section 'e' of M.I. 10. Given your work in the past, I think you may have the experience necessary."

"M.I. — Military Intelligence, is it?"

Sir O gave one of those imperceptible nods which are so perilous at auctions.

"A bit desperate for men, aren't you Sir Odbur, to be sweeping out the dregs from conshie prisons?"

"There is a certain amount of turnover in our line of endeavour, Mr Maddox. If you seek a long life expectancy, I suggest you join the R.F.C. I understand their men last some weeks, on average."

"You paint an alluring picture, Sir Odbur. I expect you have men queued up to join your merry band. Tell me, have you considered filling any of the vacancies yourself, or do you find that, like the General Staff, you have too full a schedule to visit the front lines?"

He observed me like a waxwork for an interminable time before beginning slowly to rise. "Perhaps the prospect of danger alarms you, Mr Maddox. We need speak no further of it. Good D-"

"Hold on. I'm not done listening yet."

Cranking himself back down like a scissor-jack, he assured me that M.I. 10 (e) was "not operated in the manner of Field Marshal

Haig's command. Ours is not a war of attrition. If we suffer great losses, it is from calculated risk, in circumstances in which the stakes are very high indeed."

"I would be under the command of …"

"Ultimately, the Imperial War Cabinet. Generally, under the head of Section (e)."

"Who is …?

"Myself."

"In the manner of a military command structure, I take it."

"Correct."

I took a good lungful of foetid cell while rolling the idea around, then decided.

"Your proposal is an intriguing one, Sir Odbur. However, I believe you know my mind on the subject of accepting commands."

"There would be a high degree of autonomy, in the field."

"Nevertheless. I'm afraid I can't accept orders. Offers of assignments, yes. Proposed courses of action, likewise. Commands…" I shook my head, "not, I'm afraid."

Sir Odbur rose again, decisively this time. "How disappointing," he said, extending a hand. I shook it. "Goodbye, Mr Maddox."

The days fairly breezed past after that. Between being led in irons to the exercise yard to be refreshed by a mop bucket, and being tripped-up by guards on stairs, there was no rationing of fun; like editors, they had a genius there for finding interesting ways to punctuate a sentence. In my spare moments, I amused myself articulating a rat skeleton with bits of thread. I left it — kneeling in prayer — on my dinner tray for the guard to collect, causing some small excitement. Just the usual pass-times. Until Sir Odbur returned after a fortnight. I gave him a cheery wave from where I was measuring my plank with my body, then winced.

"Good morning, Sir Odbur. You're looking tired, if you don't mind my saying so. Forgive me for not relinquishing the best seat in the usual manner. The doctors at this spa have been bruising my spleen in their attempts to correct my humours."

My visitor's lips grew even thinner. "Have you reconsidered, Mr Maddox?"

I laughed, and regretted it. "Yes, Sir Odbur. Next time, I'm going to Bath when I need a sanatorium. This one is *frightful*. Still, there may be a change of regimen soon. My guard tells me they plan to take me on holiday to sunny France, where they can pretend I'm on Active Service and shoot me when I refuse orders."

"Do you still decline my offer?" he asked.

"Of taking orders? Hmm ..." I hummed a well-known tune. My voice wasn't at its most resonant, even if the castle's cell walls had a nice echo, but I sang anyway:

"Thee haughty tyrants ne'er shall tame,
All their attempts to bend thee down
Will but arouse thy generous flame;
But work their woe, and thy renown.
Rule, Britannia! Britannia, rules the waves:
Britons never, never, never will be slaves."

Sir O shook his head with a despondent sort of air. "Not easily cowed, are you, Maddox."

"Not really, no. Nor steered. Nor bullied, either."

"Mr Maddox ... If that is your final decision." He looked uncomfortable. Perhaps he'd placed a bet with Grandfather on his chances of inducing me to join.

"It is, Sir Odbur."

"Then ... I am afraid that I am forced to accept your conditions, sir."

"Excuse me?" I said, sitting up.

"I shall make an exception. If you are agreeable to the arrangement, you will receive assignments, which you will be at liberty to undertake or reject. Should you accept an assignment, the method of its undertaking will be at your own discretion. Results are what is essential. Understand, however, that if you are captured, you may expect to be tortured and executed."

"Not much of a change, then."

"You will also frequently be operating beyond the reach of any assistance."

"It shall be just like one of those jolly expeditions to *terra incognita*. Very well, Sir Odbur. I accept."

"Excellent. We have an aeroplane ready to take you to Palestine in an hour."

I broke off from kneading my spleen. "Palestine? What, now?"

"If it is not too inconvenient. There is something happening under the Temple Mount."

"You really *are* desperate. Am I not to be trained, first? At least a pamphlet on 'How to be a Spy'?"

"There will be a dossier for you to read during the flight."

"A suit, perhaps?" I asked, smoothing my broad-arrow shirt and trousers.

"All of the necessaries will be provided. Now, if we might be on our way?" He tapped the door, summoning the guard. "I am taking the prisoner ... for special treatment. All of the paperwork has been provided to the governor, guard."

"Yessir," said the guard. "I hope you got something right special planned for *that* one."

Sir Odbur looked coldly from the guard to me, and back. "Indeed, guard. Rest assured, my man, that your *zeal*, in the execution of your duties, has not gone unnoticed."

"Thankesir!"

"Maddox? This way." Down the corridor, he asked, "You follow the club's activities, I assume?"

"Club?"

"The Etheric Explorers Club, of course. Sir Rafe has spoken of your ... assistance in his work. And yet you've never joined."

"Not much of a clubman, myself. Secret ties, and so on. A bit silly. Anyhow, the EEC is just old buffers messing about with spirit photography and that sort of thing. Not my cup of tea."

"Three of our recent casualties were members, Mr Maddox. I myself, when not serving in my capacity as Section Head of M.I. 10 (e), am treasurer."

"Ah."

After a few more steps he added, "We will maintain your conscientious objector status to allay any suspicion as to your activities."

"Ah." Well, it was probably too dangerous a job to get married on in any case.

The letter jogged out of view as my lorry plunged into yet another crater, cascading mud over the cargo and me, the solid tyres efficiently channelling the shock straight up into my spine. We were nearing the reserve trenches, the terrain turning decidedly poxy from past bombardments.

I piled into the crates of mortar-rounds when the lorry braked outside a pillbox and the driver whistled. "Your stop, mate," he called. I wondered what ever became of my old playmate from Richmond Castle. Last I heard, the guard had been suddenly declared eligible for conscription, and found himself working in the grave-digging branch of our armed services. Perhaps we'd meet again, if things went badly.

"Sergeant," I said, hailing a passing member of that species. "Detail a man to unload this crate of equipment, please, and guard it here until I am finished with your colonel."

Leaving him to his shouting, I threw everything else into my satchel, taking the big field camera itself in my other hand; I didn't fancy leaving a piece of really delicate apparatus to anyone the sergeant was likely to round up.

Inside, the commander had obviously tried to spruce up the old pill-box with a few homey touches — electric bulbs strung over the ceiling, china cups, and a walnut desk that must have taken eight men to move. Laudable efforts to be sure, if efforts doomed to failure. Even a gifted interior decorator would have difficulty achieving the comfortable, welcoming feeling of a study given a pill-box to work with.

There was a whirring sound off in one ... well, not corner, since the place was round, but say one noxious extremity of the tomb ... where a major was working away as madly as a hobgoblin in the gloom, cranking a field telephone and shouting plaintive, agitated appeals into it, like a sinner with a bad connexion to heaven. Over his desk in the centre, a stout colonel, slightly less moustachioed than the late Lord Kitchener, stopped chewing his pipe and looked up from a map. "Well?" he said. "What do *you* want?" The major stopped his shadowy organ-grinder act and looked up too. In the silence, the thump and tremor of a distant shell showered dust from the ceiling. I blew it off the camera.

"Evening, Colonel ... Major," I said, setting down my satchel. "The name's Maddox. George Maddox. Might I have a word, Colonel?"

Putting aside his pipe, the colonel took up a riding crop, regarding me with the sort of warmth that fathers hold in reserve for rank outsiders and other excrescences who come calling for their daughter's hand. I suppose in my case, "rank outsider" summed me up pretty well, had he but known at the time.

"How'd you get in here?" he demanded, stalking closer, still eyeing me with disfavour.

"Lorry, Colonel. Dashed uncomfortable things, those lorries. Should speak to someone about them. They're worse than the aeroplanes."

The colonel was now inspecting me from boots to forelocks. "What are you doing out of uniform, young man?"

It wasn't the friendly welcome one likes to receive after a trying trip. Perhaps that was what soured my mood. "What are you doing *in one*, Colonel?"

"There's a war on, blast you."

"You may take it, Colonel, that my reason is the same as yours."

"Slovenly," he complained, inspecting me further. He prodded the overflowing breast-pocket of my Mac with his little stick. "Disgraceful. Button yourself up, man."

In a blink of the colonel's rather bloodshot eyes, I snatched the crop out of his grip and tossed it away into the shadows. "Do up your own damned buttons, Colonel. I'm not in your command."

It took a few seconds of sputtering before he could say anything coherent. When he did, it was, "You're bloody well right you aren't. I won't have your sort anywhere near my command. Major! Have this man removed at once!"

The other officer rising, I shrugged. "Suit yourself, Colonel. I wasn't looking forward to my work here in any case. I must say, you have to have some high-up friends to defy the Imperial War Cabinet by tossing out a operative of M.I. 10." I unfolded my papers for him.

"What?" said the colonel, scanning the papers. The major stood awaiting developments. "Well," said the colonel, puffing indignantly, "why didn't you say you were Military Intelligence, you damned fool." He flicked his hand at the camera in mine. "Took you for one of those, you know, *journalists*, God rot them. Not that you Intelligence types aren't nearly as bad. Don't like it, having fellows outside the chain of command."

"I've been in chains before, Colonel. I didn't much like it, myself. Now, can we be getting on? I'm on a tight schedule." The civilities over with, we proceeded in a more workmanlike fashion, I explaining why I'd come. "You probably haven't heard of the first incident, up at the Somme. There was another near this sector. A new enemy weapon that sliced up a whole company. At a salient. There was a survivor in the most recent attack."

"That? You're not investigating *that?* The man was clearly shell-shocked. Went on about knights in armour wiping out his company." The colonel's interest turned to contempt when he saw that I wasn't about to contradict him. "What next? Will M.I. be investigating the Angels of Mons?" He sat, disgustedly shaking his head and stuffing his pipe with tobacco.

There didn't seem much profit in pursuing the point, particularly as our analysis of the angels was still inconclusive.

"The unknown weapon," I continued, "has yet to be reliably described and analysed. My assignment is to observe it in action. From the pattern of use, such as it is with only two attacks thus far, we predict it will be deployed against the salient in your line tonight. I will be photographing it when it is. Your coöperation would be appreciated. As there is no known countermeasure, I suggest that it would be prudent to withdraw all but a skeleton force from the firing line and prepare to launch a counter-assault when the follow-up shock troops arrive after the deployment of the Weapon. Have our artillery ranged to give them a welcome."

He puffed, on his pipe this time. "Out of the question. If you knew the losses we took, taking that salient. No. We'll re-enforce the line. They won't get by. That's C Company ... colonial troops up there. Highlanders. Canadians. The Huns will think twice when they see what they're up against. I'll order more machine guns for Captain Peacocke. He's OC C Company. Your *knights*," he said, smirking beneath his moustache, "won't get past a company of our Highlanders armed with Lewis guns."

I did my best to make him understand that we were up against something unusually potent, as bad as tanks, only managing to get the further concession of star-shells and artillery on call for the attack.

"I will expect a full report of your observations, Maddox," said the colonel at the end of our conference. "The private guarding your equipment, he'll show you up to the salient."

I picked up my satchel. "Are you sure you wouldn't like to get a first-hand look for yourself, Colonel?"

He wagged his pipe in a negative. "Your job, Maddox. Not mine."

"It would do the men no end of good, Colonel. They like to know the brass take their turn in the slaughter. It would boost morale."

"Just get on with it, man."

"One last thing," I said, taking an envelope from my pocket. He looked up irritably from the map that had already taken back his attention. "May I ask, Colonel, that if I fail to return, you would see that this letter is sent to my fiancée?"

He nodded, and I started to go.

"Maddox," he said, turning me back. "What do think this weapon is, really?"

"I haven't the foggiest, Colonel. I only know that it is something very unpleasant indeed, and that it will be arriving tonight. Good day, gentlemen."

Outside, the private — a big bald chap who probably bent iron bars as a hobby in his off hours — was standing guard over my gear.

"Off we go, Private. Take me to C Company, please."

He led the way with the larger of the luggage, up the communications trenches connecting the reserve, support, and front lines. It was slow going, not because Froggatt (that was the private's name) was flagging under the weight of my equipment — the man was indefatigable. The duck-boards of the trenches, even when they weren't entirely covered in slippery rats the size of beavers, weren't built for efficiently moving the masses, and there was a good deal of sidestepping and waiting while the opposing traffic passed. I pointed this out to private Froggatt during one of our stops. He lit a cigarette while a blanket-covered stretcher passed, going west.

"Inefficient, don't you think, Private?"

"Sir?"

"These single-lane communications trenches. They should

double them, like busy highways. Have one lane for traffic frontward, another for the rearward flow."

The private pondered this proposal, picking up the gear again. "Wouldn't work, sir," he said, around his cigarette. "Too hard to defend, y'see. Twice as many enemy could reach the next line."

We started frontward again. "No, no, Private. You don't know the German mind. We'd simply put 'One Way' arrows on the communications trenches. No German is capable of acting contrary to a street sign."

Froggatt laughed. "Problem is, sir, the Canadians'd pay no attention to the signs, whatever they said, so you'd get them coming and going in both trenches, and they're too polite to pass anybody. The trenches'd fill up with 'em, all saying, 'Sorry, I'll move, you go by first,' and 'No, you go first,' and 'No, really, you pass, I can wait,' and before you knew it the war'd be over and no-one would've budged so much as a foot."

I hadn't anticipated this obstacle. It presented a vivid picture. "Rather like that anyway, isn't it, Froggatt?"

"Amen, sir." he said.

In the fullness of God's good time we arrived at the OC's dugout on the firing line, with no man's land just a (parlous) hop beyond the parapet. The private set down my gear and cracked his neck.

"Well, Froggatt, we part ways here." I dug a wad of grubby one, two, and five-lira banknotes out of one of my pockets and foisted them on him. "Here's a little tip for excellent service. You can probably get them exchanged on your next leave. There must be a pound's worth or two there. Won't need them where I'm going."

"Thank you, sir. Don't get yourself down, though, sir. Plenty of fellahs survive a spell in the front line."

I shook my head disapprovingly. "You are a pessimist, aren't you, Froggatt. I meant I won't be going back to Italy any time soon. God knows where they'll send me after his. Cheerio, Private."

There was no Captain Peacocke in the dugout, however, only a lieutenant replacing a telephone receiver. The place was rather starker than the colonel's opulent pill-box, the only decoration be-

ing a calendar of Lord Kitchener affixed to a sand bag with a bayonet. Noticing once more his Lordship's resemblance to the colonel, I marvelled at how a man like Kitchener could have drowned
with that vast moustache to buoy him up. He probably used too
much wax, or not enough Lifebuoy soap. "Are you Maddox?" the
lieutenant asked. I acknowledged the fact. "You can find the Captain that way," he said, pointing northish.

Leaving the gear, I headed off in the direction named until I
discovered a clean-shaven chap with a football, and three pips on
his shoulder; a healthy specimen of junior officer, with the right
amount of chin — enough to look human without going overboard
into Mr Punch territory.

"Captain Peacocke, I presume?" I said, just as he tossed the
ball up into the air. A few of his men were lounging about on fire
steps or standing, taking in their leader's exhibition of sportsman-
ship. While the ball was airborne, Peacocke flicked his hand in a
greeting or request for patience before catching the ball and tossing it again.

"Tin hat," he said to me. "Get one on." He nodded to one of his
men, who brought me a helmet that I screwed snugly into place.

"Captain, I …"

"In a second." He kept tossing the football. Obviously they
were starved for amusement in the long hours of front-line service,
unless this were one of those superstitious rituals that soldiers in-
vent to guard themselves from harm. I was about to point out that
the feet were more generally considered the proper members to use
in football, and offer to demonstrate, when a bullet shot overhead
and spent itself in the mud of the parados at the back of the trench.

Peacocke kept lobbing the football into the air at irregular
intervals, now accompanied by regular enemy fire, like an Air
Corps balloon-busting mission in miniature. I watched, fascinated,
as the football went up and down hypnotically, with bangs. This
fun-with-the-Hun continued for quite a few tosses, until a much
louder 'crack' sounded a little ways away, past the traverse in the
line where the trench zigzagged out of sight. Peacocke essayed a
few more tosses without any incoming fire.

"Easily bored, these *Boche*," I observed.

Rapid footfalls preceded a corporal around the bend in the

trench. He carried a rifle with telescopic sights. "Got the bastard," he said, with a sort of subdued, grim triumph.

"Good show, Trotter," said Peacocke. He tossed me the ball. "Hun sniper," he explained. "Got our Private McNeil, just now, so we decided the bugger had overstayed his welcome on this section of line. Now, at least, I can write to McNeil's Mum that his killer didn't outlive him long. If that will be any consolation for her."

"Hard luck for McNeil," I said, sympathetically. Snipers were a cruel source of surprises.

"May you have better luck with his helmet. Now, who the hell are you, anyhow?"

I decided I liked this Captain Peacocke.

Back in his dugout, I filled him in on the visitors who'd be arriving, most likely, that evening, revealing selections of the intelligence dossier and explaining that in the other attacks, the weapon was followed fifteen minutes later by heavily-armed storm troops who leapfrogged over our former front-line to make a push deeper. "Thus far, they've made limited used of the Weapon. Presumably the attacks have been trials on vulnerable salients, with the assault troops ensuring that no witnesses survived to inform us of the nature of the Weapon."

"Some kind of new tank? Or could they be mutilating the bodies to give the impression of a new weapon?" wondered Peacocke. "I've seen men torn apart in more ways than I can name, but never chopped up like this," he said of the post-attack photograph. "How do we counter it?"

That was a question that had been much on my mind since I received the dossier. "Unknown. My mission is simply to get a picture of the Weapon in action, since there are no reliable reports of it. The nails puzzle me as well. If the Germans can supply their assault teams with automatic weapons, flame-throwers, and so on, it hardly seems likely they would need to resort to crude nail-bombs. Whatever the case, it is a safe assumption that there is something very unusual about this weapon."

"Based," asked Lt. Drummond, who was still present in the dugout, "on the casualties?"

"Based on the fact that I'm here. An ordinary weapon would have drawn a different section of M.I. 10."

Officially, I was being remiss in my duty of secrecy to discuss intelligence details with minor local officers; they might be captured and reveal what we knew. However, what we knew amounted to an anthill of information that the enemy already *knew* we knew. And the pattern of attack hadn't included taking prisoners.

Peacocke rubbed his chin, leaving a burgeoning goatee of mud on it. "I'd be inclined to fall back to the supply trench, range our artillery on this line, and let them sneak into a maelstrom. I would, if I hadn't received orders to the contrary. We're getting some heavy weaponry and two more companies in reserve."

"I suggested falling back to your colonel. He wouldn't have it."

"Yes," said Peacocke. "He's a member of the *l'offensive à outrance* school of thought."

"Mmm. I noticed something of the offensive spirit in him."

The officers nodded. We sat in silence for a while, thinking the problem over. I could see no other sensible way to proceed, so I proposed my idea.

"Strictly speaking, gentlemen, my job here is to snap a few photographs of the weapon prior to scuttling off. Your role, of course, is to be chopped up like the last two companies. Before you decide to do so, I would invite you to cast a glance over this letter," I said, withdrawing the document from my satchel. It was from the Imperial War Cabinet requesting, in His Majesty's name, whom it might concern to lend any and all assistance to the bearer, George Maddox, in the performance of his duties.

"Yes?" said Peacocke, after looking it over. "What do you want us to do for you?"

"Clear out. You're in my way."

"What? You mean, withdraw to the supply trench?"

"Precisely. I can't get a photograph of this thing if I have a company of men milling about my camera being chopped into highlander hash. I just need one man to take the first plate and leg it out of here while I expose the second plate. That way, we're bound to get at least one picture of the thing. Then, when I make a run for it with the second plate, you can send everything you have at the front line, and signal for a bombardment of no man's land to do in the Hun assault troops."

Peacocke and Drummond talked it over between themselves,

raising a few more objections to the plan until everything was sorted out, pretty much as I had suggested (naturally I left the tactical side to them). The only variation was that Peacocke insisted on staying with me in the front line.

"This is my command. I'm staying. I'll get Trotter to be your runner. He's reliable."

"Fine. Perhaps we can give our uninvited guests a surprise. *L'audace, encore de l'audace, toujours de l'audace*, I always say. To be fair, Danton said it before I did."

Peacocke nodded in agreement. "Yes. Of course, he lost his head eventually, didn't he."

With the trench too busy with men moving out, I assembled the camera in the dugout. It seemed the case contained more delicate equipment than I'd thought — a French flash system that looked like a collection of jam jars stuffed with magnesium tape was housed snugly in its own compartment. It was mostly connected in the correct shape by the time Peacocke reappeared in the dugout doorway.

"We're ready. Got the ends of this area barricaded to keep the Weapon contained. Get your camera set up while there's still light."

Out in the trench, the gloaming was fading, the sun having gone west not long ago. Perhaps I'd be following it before too long. At the "T" intersection of the firing line and the communication trench I dug the tripod legs in and aimed the camera down the trench towards the next traverse, around which a lamp had been hung to silhouette anyone rounding the corner. It would be moonless, with nothing but starlight, and that only if the sky cleared. If, as it inevitably would, fate made the Weapon appear in the opposite direction, the camera could swivel.

"Right," said Peacocke. "Now we wait, I suppose." He and the corporal installed themselves into a fire-step on one side of the camera with a Lewis Gun, several drums of ammunition, and a rifle between them. I settled in comfortably on another fire-step — or as comfortable as you can get in a ditch into which certain death is soon going to drop without warning — armed with a Thermos and a Webley flare pistol. The little brass blunderbuss was for signalling for star shells and a bombardment just beyond our front line.

"Coffee?" I suggested.

"This," said Peacocke from the other side of the tripod, "might not be the best time to brew up a pot, I think."

"No, I mean I have a Thermos of coffee if you care for some."

Cpl. Trotter trotted off and brought back some tin mugs, into which I decanted Thermos № 2.

"Hell," said Trotter, after sipping his. "That's some good coffee."

"Mm," agreed Peacocke. "Not like the dirt we get. Obviously M.I. has its perquisites, eh, Maddox?"

"If you must know," I said, after a sip of the now no longer piping-hot but still delicious coffee, "it's Italian coffee. That is, it was brewed in Italy earlier today."

"Ah, the life of Military Intelligence. Must be nice," said Peacocke.

"You're welcome to make the trip yourself, if you're that desperate for a cup. Personally, I found flying backwards through the Alps in a freezing open cockpit a high price to pay for good coffee, particularly as that model of plane has an unfortunate habit of shedding its wings when it's feeling cranky."

They grunted, enjoying their coffee without further complaint. I flicked on my Orilux torch and returned to Amanda's interrupted letter.

Peacocke's voice came out of the gloom. "You should turn that off. Destroys your night vision."

"We've hours left in our vigil before any excitement. They've been raiding well past midnight, and the Hun isn't given to whimsical changes of routine."

> *I know,* continued Amanda, *mother and father —
> and our friends — will understand eventually ...
> after the war.*

She was in the know, naturally. Sir Odbur wouldn't have approved of my telling her that I was actually in the employ of M.I., rather than a conshie taking the grand tour to avoid ridicule and imprisonment at home. One can't allow oneself to drift into the paranoid morass of suspecting the whole world. If one can't trust one's fiancée, who can one trust?

I tucked my boots up onto the fire-step, as a rat had started chewing on them.

> *If it ends. The longer it goes on, the more poisoned the world grows, as if we've become a mob of angry rooks calling for the blood of anyone who speaks against the will of the flock. That is why I am so glad that you are doing what you are doing, even if it is terribly dangerous, George. If we are doomed to act as a mob, relinquishing our individuality to the crowd, the sooner our common will can be directed toward building instead of destruction, the better for the world.*

Amanda was a lot like Melissa in her views. Of course, they'd been pals a long time.

"What are you doing over there, anyway," asked Peacocke.

I sighed. One expects interruptions in wartime, but not pestering. "I am reading letters, if you must know. Private, personal letters."

"Ah."

My pondering of the question of whether Amanda was an optimist or a pessimist was disturbed again in a few moments.

"The colonel," said Peacocke, "says we get" (and here he put on a kind of obese, dentured, brass-hat sort of voice) "*indolent, melancholy, and distracted*, when we read our letters. So he holds them in the rear until we go off front line duty. The last post is still in a bag back in the supply trench."

Trotter muttered something mutinous, but largely unintelligible.

"What's that?" I asked.

"He says Mrs Trotter sent him a Dundee cake," interpreted Peacocke. "And he's fretting over it."

"I can well imagine, Trotter. Many's the crisis I've been in, when I bethought myself that a good slab of fruitcake would improve the outlook to no end. Your colonel's an ass."

To keep the evening from waxing melancholy and distracted, I passed over the bottle of *grappa*. "Have a snort of this. It's not

Dundee cake, but it takes the chill off."

It did, for a while. Until — I checked my luminous watch — 3:15. The trench had been deathly quiet since it was evacuated, without even the usual sporadic sniper fire at intervals to enliven the monotony. Then something broke the spell, a slithering and a crash like a dead horse sliding into a pit of trash. Damp and rheumatic now, I sprang off the fire step, turning the camera towards the sound. The others were on their feet as well. Silence fell again, long enough that I began wondering if part of the trench had simply collapsed from subsidence. Then there was another cracking splash from the same direction, and another, seeming to echo from both ends of trench. I pulled back the dark-slide covering the photographic plate. The noises — colossal footsteps they had to be — were getting louder, riveting the three of us to the faint light leaking around the bend of the trench. There was no question. It had to be the Weapon. I aimed the Webley at the black sky and fired a flare.

The Weapon passed the corner just as the flare snuffed itself out in a crump hole in no man's land somewhere. It was a man. A huge man, silhouetted.

"Jesus," said Trotter. "Must be ten feet tall."

Well, nine maybe.

"Shut your eyes!" I told them, following the advice myself an instant before I opened the shutter and set off the flash. Even through my eyelids I could see the burst of light. It must have blinded the Weapon, if there was anything human about it.

Slamming the slide back over the plate, I whisked it out and shoved it into Trotter's hands, the first of the star shells I'd summoned choosing that moment to burst high over our heads.

"Get out of here, Trotter," I told him, and pushed another plate into the camera. Trotter vanished down the communications trench with my evidence. Ejecting the spent flash, I fumbled another into its reflector dish. The thing was still coming, marching through a welter of living shadows that moved in a drunken nightmare, cast by the star-shells that were sliding around the sky on their own weird ecliptics in their own sped-up time, like years of moons all crammed into a moment. Its legs were smashing through the duck boards into the mire below with every step. God knows how much it weighed.

"That poor bastard," I muttered, thinking of the lone survivor of the raids. "It really is a knight."

I could see now that the Weapon was wielding a sword, one too big for any man to swing — hence the minced company. A shield, too.

There was a clatter as Peacocke threw the bolt on the Lewis Gun. A moment later it erupted in a racket that went on for about ten seconds, lighting up the Weapon's shield like a firework pinwheel until the Lewis gun was left smoking in a ringing fug of cordite, magazine empty and shell-catcher bag chiming with spent brass; a maelstrom of fire like that would have torn a person to pieces. The Weapon kept coming.

Peacocke swapped magazines, for whatever good that would do. The Weapon was only steps away now. One more picture, and we could make a dash for it. For the sake of curiosity, I shouted.

"*Halt! Stillgestanden!*"

Surprisingly, it worked. Peacocke and I looked at each other, then back to the stock-still, monstrous knight.

"*Danke schön,*" I said, as it was being so considerate. "Now, smile please!"

Click, flash, and that was that, another job well done.

"Time to be beetling off," I told Peacocke, and whisked the plate out of the camera. Or would have, if my sleeve hadn't caught in the camera knobs or some other annoying projection, launching me into what must have looked like a furious tango with the tripod. Try as I might, I couldn't untangle myself.

"What the hell are you playing at!" demanded Peacocke, not without reason. The Weapon was upon us, about to cut in to my dance. It loomed over the camera like death personified, or like a very impassive doorman about to eject a member of the press. I was trying to decide between further ignoble struggle or giving up hope, when another star shell lit the Weapon, revealing its expressionless face, its armour, the thousands of nail heads studding it, and its huge shield. The shield was embossed with tall, Teutonic letters: *ROLAND*.

"Good Lord," I mumbled, "*Child Rowland to the dark tower came/His word was still Fie, foh, and fum/I smell the blood of a British man.*"

I don't think Roland approved of the verse, for he ran me through with the eight-foot broadsword.

At least, I assume that was what he was trying for. The sword (possibly named "Durandal", but probably not), had gone through the mess of camera gear, through my Mac, and had stuck in the massive oaken beams that were shoring up the trench wall. The ensuing scene was, as you can imagine, fraught with awkwardness. I wriggled like an uncoöperative entomological specimen. Peacocke was dumbstricken at our guest's *faux pas*. Roland himself wore a look of bafflement, insofar as he was capable of any expression. Possibly he had never experienced this particular difficulty before in what, for the sake of convenience, we shall call his life.

What concerned me most, to be perfectly honest, was that when Peacocke finally snapped out of his daze, he demonstrated that he was back in play by shoving a Mills bomb into a chink in Roland's armour, and hammering it in further with the butt of his Lewis gun. In retrospect, I suppose he must have assumed that with a blade of that size transfixing me I was not long for this world in any case, but at the time I felt that his actions with the Mills bomb showed such a singular lack of consideration for my feelings that when Roland, too, came to his senses and took a swipe at the captain, knocking him base over apex, I thought it a not entirely unwelcome development.

I redoubled my furious wriggling when the sword began uttering squeaks suggestive of steel working free of oak. Roland — now looking a trifle *furioso* himself — was putting his weight into it when, in another unexpected development, all of Amanda's letters shot out of my open pocket and plastered themselves onto the knight's face, the writing on them vanishing as they struck him. With a great and undignified effort, I exploited the distraction by squirming free of my Mac, snatching the pin from the Mills bomb *en route*.

Peacocke was staggering groggily to his feet, so I shoved him 'round the bend into the communications trench as Roland, irked by his stuck sword, fired a volley of nails at us that whiffled past like a flight of birds, catching my tin hat as well as a shoulder blade that I had been quite fond of. Then Roland exploded.

I didn't pause to check on his condition, I steered Peacocke away from the firing line until we reached the column of Highlanders who'd been so recently pulled out, queued up now in the communications trench. Trotter was at the head of the line.

"Why," I panted, "aren't you in the supply trench with my plate?"

He swung an arm towards his fellows. "Too crowded. They handed it back."

Well, I hoped they had. I'd lost the second plate in the wreckage of the tripod, making it the only evidence to come out of this show. I checked my watch. 3:22. Eight minutes until the assault team arrived to mop us up.

"Where's your lieutenant, Drummond?"

"Here, sir," came a voice from the murky depths.

"I've lost my flare gun. Have you yours?"

"Yes, sir."

"Fire it for the bombardment."

In another minute all hell broke loose — or, a normal day on the front line. Shells showered no man's land in a deafening din, peppering us with mud and sand from a hundred yards away. Impressive, if unlikely to stop a company or two of shock troops. We needed to reoccupy the firing line within minutes. And Roland might not have been alone.

"He's all right," I told the lieutenant, who was trying to get sense out of Peacocke. "Only shaken up."

"Sir," said Trotter. "Sir, I think I've seen one of those things before."

"The knight? You were attacked?"

"No, sir. One of the Heinies we captured one time had this picture postcard on him. It was of this statue thing, all pounded full of nails. Called it a 'noggle manner', whatever the hell that is. Said it was a fund-raiser for their war effort. You paid into the war chest for the chance to pound a nail into the thing."

It was like everything stopped for a moment. I felt a kind of wave … of fever. And then I shouted down the line. "The last post! Pass the mail bag up here … hurry!"

I can't say I thought it — it was one of those flashes, where everything falls into place faster than the mind can follow. I pieced it together later.

Word passed faster than a runner down the trench, and in three minutes the last post was passing over heads from hand to hand until the lumpy canvas bag was tossed to me by Trotter. My watch said 3:25 — five minutes until the real show opened.

"Have you got your senses back?" I asked Peacocke.

"I'm all right. What do you suggest?"

"Pick ten men with heavy weapons and grenades, and follow me."

Sorting all that out in fifteen seconds in a dark trench could have been a débâcle, worse even than my tripod tango, had they not been such a disciplined body of men, and for the first time in my life I thanked God that events weren't in the hands of a crowd of people like me. Peacocke, Trotter, myself, and nine men clanking like a many-footed armoury moved forward, back into the firing trench, with Lt. Drummond commanding the rest of the company; if all went well they would take up defensive positions along the line as we cleared it of Weapons. We were there in seconds, with the bombardment still screaming and the earth still trembling, the star shells still preternaturally bright in the sky.

Even as we reached the firing line, two of Drummond's men pushed past carrying a heavy Vickers gun, mounting a small redoubt at the intersection from which they immediately poured fire into no man's land. I spied our old chum Roland then, sadly declined since we'd last met. He was a sort of mess of arms and legs, still moving like a dying crab, while his sword stuck harmlessly in the wall. The thought of him snatching hold of anyone's leg was not attractive, though, so I got as close as I dared before plucking a handful of letters from the post bag, flinging them over the ruined Roland. Again, as with Amanda's letters, they plastered themselves to his body with a kind of magnetism, provoking a wild fit. In the nick of time, it occurred to me to holler "Down!" Nails flew in all directions, not a few of them burying themselves in the mail bag that I ducked behind. Then Roland, or what was left of him, went still. For a few seconds I hesitated over which way to go next. More men were already mounting the fire-steps and firing Lewis guns or rifle grenades over the parapet.

"Give me some mail," said Peacocke. He took an armful from the bag and headed north with five of the men, leaving Trotter, me, and the rest to take the other branch. The rest of the company was splitting up at the intersection, going either Peacock's way or mine. I set off, thankful I'd taken to wearing cavalry boots (sans spurs), for the duck-boards were in a frightful state following our chum Roland's passage. It was a harrowing journey, I don't mind telling you, for even without checking my watch I knew our time was up. The enemy would be dropping in any second, keen to make merry, while meeting a nine-foot inhuman knight at any corner was a peril not to be sneezed at either. By the time we'd negotiated forty yards of mud and splinters my nerves were in a worse state than my shirt, and I was wishing there'd been the time — and the pliers — to pull the nail out of my back.

In the end, the thing came to meet us as I was wallowing through a wet pit at the bottom of the trench. It was practically a twin of our Roland — Roland II if you will. A few of the fellows at my back took pot-shots at it, if you can call emptying a couple of magazines-full of .303 rounds over my head "taking pot-shots". Possibly I should have explained the procedure to them. Roland II weathered the blaze of jacketed lead with the usual contempt, so I dug into the post bag and flung letters at him, no doubt much to the amazement again of my little half-section. They stuck to the knight rather like stamps on a colossal parcel, making him almost at once go wobbly, pawing to get them off.

"On the ground," I told the men. I dug into the mail for another wad of letters, only to find I'd taken hold of a box. It was addressed to the corporal.

"I'm afraid it's your parcel, Trotter old man," I said over my shoulder to where he was flattened in the muck and splinters.

"Do it, sir," he said, and never have I been more proud of British pluck. For it was certainly his long-awaited Dundee cake. I nodded, and hurled the parcel at Roland II, and damn me if that Dundee cake didn't shear Childe Roland's head clean off his shoulders. The headless trunk thrashed about a bit, until I hurled another mass of letters at it, whereupon it spat out a little flurry of nails, then gave up the ghost. Or whatever it had to give up.

"My word, Trotter," I said when it seemed safe to get up, "but your missus bakes a fierce cake."

"Yes, sir," he said.

Alas, poor cakeless Trotter.

In the assault that followed — there not being a large role reserved
for a civilian armed with an empty mailbag — I played only the
most minor part, mostly consisting of keeping out of the way of
the people who knew what they were doing. More out of cour-
tesy than for any practical contribution I could make to the battle
with it, Drummond gave me his revolver when he discovered me
loafing about the trench, practising my skill at contortionism as
I strove to extract the nail from my scapula; he had a Lewis gun
himself, and from the way its barrel was sizzling in the drizzle
he'd been making good use of it. As it happened, the revolver did
prove to be of material assistance later when a rather crazed chap
dropped in around five a.m. I can't altogether blame him for his
mood, for if he'd been out between the lines for a couple of hours
being bombed and machine-gunned when he'd been expecting a
peaceful saunter to a trench full of dead men, he must have been
sorely disappointed by the conditions. That didn't entirely excuse
him for roaring at me as he leapt into the trench, nor for trying to
bayonet me. He calmed down by the time I ran out of ammunition,
and his rifle made me a rather more serviceable weapon in the
circumstances than an empty Webley.

After that there was a heavy bombardment on the trench, which
I assumed was laid on by the Germans, though with our generals
one could never be sure. About dawn, when things settled down
and the wounded had been carried away to casualty stations, I
found my way back to the wreckage of my camera carrying Roland
II's slightly offended-looking head, where I discovered the greatest miracle of the whole affair: the *grappa* bottle, unbroken and
unemptied. Only giant monsters and a battalion of shock troops (or
perhaps strict Presbyterianism) could have saved a bottle of liquor
in a trench-full of Canadian Highlanders.

I installed myself on the narrow fire-step, back against the mud
wall, watching in a sleepless, dreamlike way the men coming and
going. An especially grubby one halted.

"Maddox," he said. It was Peacocke. "Not dead, then."

"If you say so. Have some *grappa*."

"Don't mind if I do. Makes a nice change from grog."

When we'd had our first sips, he asked me, "You know what your problem is, Maddox?"

I nodded, sadly, trying in vain to wriggle into a more comfortable position. "Yes. I've got a bloody great Hun nail stuck in my back that I can't reach. It's like a curse, or something."

"Your problem," he continued, oblivious, "is that you're a leader who doesn't have any followers."

I poured another slosh of *grappa*. "Childe Roland clouted you on the head too hard."

"I'm serious."

"Thought you were a grouse, or a capercaillie, or a peacock, or …"

"Don't go changing the subject … But maybe I *was* knocked silly. If I remember rightly, we killed four walking statues with a bag of mail."

"Yes. You should probably forget that. I should imagine it's classified *Most Secret*."

"But what …"

"What was it?" I said. At last there was leisure to work through the details. "It wasn't a man, obviously. Or a machine. Trotter put me onto the answer when he mentioned the post card he'd seen. Though I wouldn't have known what to do about had it not been for Amanda's letters, and their hurling themselves into the breach, as it were. The Rolands, and whatever other form the things take, were a focus for the will of a whole nation. Thousands of people hammered nails into them, hammering in their will to win, too. My grandfather would call it 'imprinting a quantum of will on Roland's etheric signature'; you can think of it as putting a little of their souls into the thing. All of them with the same urge: victory."

"Jesus," said Peacocke.

"Indeed."

"And you do this all the time?"

"It certainly feels like it."

"But, what was that business with the mail?"

"Well, it's only guesswork. But I think it's the same thing, really. The post was also a collective will to win. Or no, not that exactly. A lot of individual wills. Every letter is a wish, to see someone again. Every card is a hope they'll come back. I think the letters and the nails neutralized each other, like opposite charges. Like some kind of etheric rock-paper-scissors."

"The girl behind the man behind the gun," said Peacocke.

"Or behind the cake, in Trotter's case."

"Pity about that cake."

"Indeed. I haven't eaten since I was in Italy."

"What, you mean you flew all that way without even a snack?"

"I know," I said. "That's modern transportation for you."

I think I rambled on for some time, speculating as to the nature of the Rolands. I'm not sure, since I fell asleep at some point. Whatever the case, the Weapon wouldn't trouble us any more, not now that there was an effective countermeasure. Which reminded me to leave word with the colonel that I'd be recommending to the I.W.C. that all postal deliveries be distributed upon arrival, and that if he knew what was good for his career he'd start doing so at once. Also, I needed to get my final letter back from him before he decided I was dead and posted it to Amanda.

There was something shaking me when I woke up, some hours later. At first I thought it was another bombardment, and that I'd gone deaf, but it was only a goggled despatch rider covered in leather and mud.

"You Maddox?" he asked.

I sighed. "I'm afraid so."

He handed over a new despatch box. Inside was ...

"Oh, bugger." They wanted me ... in *Petrograd*.

"Good news?"

"Why can't a crisis ever happen on the Côte d'Azur?" Then I cheered up, remembering it wasn't an order. I needed at least a day to clean up and get a few hours sleep. Why *not* pop down to the Côte d'Azur for a few days? Someone else could handle this show, someone ...

Trotter nodded as he staggered by under a load of new duckboards.

They weren't getting a break. None of them were. I threw together my few bits of luggage.

"Before we set off," I said to the courier, "have a go at pulling this nail out of my back, would you? There's a good chap."

The Grinsfield Penitent

Father Drewitt was leant against one of the church buttresses, sheltering his smouldering Woodbine from a November mist that had been falling long enough to coat the jumbled old tombstones of the churchyard until they and their grisled lichen glistened in the grey light. He felt as worn as the sandstone. Armistice Day always recalled for Drewitt that first November 11th of memory; the first Armistice Day. It had rained that day, too, on the officers wearily assuring their men as they met them along the line, again, and again, that it was not another rumour.

It was really going to end this time.

How easily they could believe then that it would go on for eternity, as Hell should, when the view past the parapet was of the same ruined fields that had met the regiment four years earlier, the regiment that was the same in name, even if the bodies had changed.

Hell. Much of the time they'd been ten feet below Hell, in dugouts. They'd had to climb a ladder to get up to Hell.

The field had only been more ruined in '18, and better manured with the Empire's youth, that last generation of Victorians. Sometimes it seemed to Drewitt that he had personally performed last rites upon the whole generation. He certainly had given them to one boy, a lung-wounded sniper-target who, as he lay drowning upon his stretcher on the 11th, twenty years ago, red froth on his lips, had stared hard with more than a mute pain — with a hurt look of bewilderment. "But, they said it was over," his face seemed to protest still.

A gentler rattle came up the lane, of a loose mudguard, and of muttering spokes choked with leaves. Stapleton, the thin young priest from Lower Chiddinghurst. For their regular Friday mutual confession. Drewitt dropped his cigarette to join its fallen fellows, and shrugged off through the drizzle to meet Stapleton at the church door. Drewitt offered no greetings as the other wrestled with his kickstand, but led the way inside.

The programme of light music on the battery wireless echoed in the empty church; had they been on the mains, he would have installed an electric fire for days like this, to drive the deathly chill from the air. When Stapleton arrived, he shook a rain-shower from his overcoat onto the stone flags, checked the white poppy in his buttonhole, and laid the coat over the back of a pew.

"Bitter day," said Stapleton, as he rubbed life back into his hands. He nodded, approvingly, at the identical white poppy on Drewitt's coat. "Did you have time to read the PPU material I sent?"

Drewitt inclined his head to the shelf by door, where what looked like several weeks' letters were heaped. Probably the Peace Pledge Union pamphlets were in there somewhere. "Haven't sorted though the post recently."

The only one he'd opened was a letter from Roberts, an old friend in Canada. Or, Sir Charles, as he was now. Roberts was going to address a university somewhere named Guelph with his poem "Peace with Dishonour", which he'd composed in response to the Munich Agreement. Even remembering the gas attacks, and mucking through a vast cemetery turned inside out, Drewitt too had a sour taste from Munich. Better, thought Roberts, to endure the passing horrors of war, which hurt but heal, than "long dishonour, brief cowed peace, / For freedom stripped and cast to the loud pack / This stain endures."

Stapleton frowned fastidiously at the disordered mail, and noticed the boxes piled in the shadows. Though he never confessed to coveting St Cuthman's, Drewitt sensed a proprietorial interest whenever the other priest visited.

"I know," acknowledged Drewitt, "Looks as if God's moving house, doesn't it." *God knows, I'd understand if He did.* "They're finally working on that ruined roof on my cottage. Had to move my things in here out of the rain."

"Well, it won't be for long, I suppose," said Stapleton, in what sounded irritatingly like a personal dispensation. "Though, it must be almost as damp in here." He went over to the pile and returned a book to its box from where it had tumbled onto the flags, pulling out a framed photograph as he did. "Do you play? Football, I mean?"

Stepping closer, Drewitt remembered the picture before seeing it. "Ah. That. I was behind the camera, not in the team." A cluster of men of various shapes and sizes, in uniform, were standing and crouching. One had a football. "That's at the front. 1914. Do you notice anything about it?"

The wireless concert ended while Stapleton regarded the photo, the BBC filling the silence with the hourly news. *This is London calling ... Reich Minister Goebbels announced today that the German government would be putting an end to the anti-Jewish pogroms that have swept his country since the assassination by Herschel Grynszpan in Paris of Ernst von Rath, Third Secretary of the German Embassy in Paris...*

A closer examination failed to prove illuminating. "No. Should I ...?"

... His Majesty's Government's official protest of the violence, Prime Minister Chamberlain has assured the British public that the peace guaranteed by the Munich Agreement is not threatened by recent unrest...

If both sides had only shot their generals the day of that photograph, it really might have been over at Christmas. But then, generals rarely get within rifle range of the front. "Look again. Half of them are German."

"Oh yes. The Christmas Truce, was it?"

Christmas. Had both camps thought God was on their side that Christmas, as they sang carols in no-man's land, or had that dreadful certainty come later, as they fell into an abyss that seemed to have no end, as a way of justifying the slaughter and the sacrifice with more slaughter, more sacrifice?

Drewitt dug out his pack of Woodbines and lit one, the profanity of the act silently nettling the other priest. Taking the photo, Drewitt let his eyes drift over the faces until the ash fell from his cigarette. Stapleton fidgeted.

"That's Tremane," said Drewitt, pointing a glowing ember at a man in a peaked cap with a stick. "Our lieutenant. Took a First in Maths at Oxford. Went west in '15. The burial parties never found a body. Just gone. Just gone." They all were now. Probably even the Jerries. Drewitt switched off the wireless.

"The PPU," said Stapleton, "will make sure we don't make the same mistake again. You will speak about your experiences, when we motor up to London with the other members for the meeting?"

"It must not. It cannot happen like that again."

"The War was a great trial for you, wasn't it, Father Drewitt," said Stapleton, drawing upon the limited stock of sympathetic phrases with which the seminary equips young priests.

"We rarely choose our trials. Only how we face them." And Drewitt had chosen badly. So very badly. "Shall we confess?" he suggested, stamping out the cigarette against the flags and moving with echoing steps through the nave towards the confessional, remembering a day twenty-five years before, and a visitor.

According to the Sussex county guidebook, 1899 edition, Father Drewitt's little sandstone church was not lacking in attractions for the modern traveller. There was the narrow, sunken country lane, overhung with a picturesque guard of stately oaks and elms — upstanding citizens of the Weald that lent the holy place a mild and dappled shade in the summer, and a romantic air for the rest of the year. St. Cuthman's crypt could boast use, at one time, as a warehouse for the smugglers who had sneaked brandy past the King's revenue men to warm the livers and lights of London's roistering forefathers. An altar tomb offered a quite pleasing effigy of a minor crusader in armour, comfortably reposed across the lid after his holy labours in the Levant. And naturally there was a ghost. Clearly, a destination well worth both the journey and the suggested donation of sixpence (historical booklet included). Surpassing even these not undistinguished attractions, the church gloried in a single outstanding virtue which raised it in the estimation of travellers and antiquarians alike above all the surrounding Church of England edifices, noble as many of them were in artistic or historical merit: unlike the established churches, Roman St. Cuthman's was not locked up tight for six days of the week, and even left its doors invitingly ajar in clement weather.

No, if St. Cuthman's lacked something, it was parishioners. The village was old, the residents seemingly even older. Youth had succumbed, either to war, or to the the Sirens of the city: the electric light, the telephone, and the weekly wage. The excitement. The forgetfulness of fashion. Grinsfield was a shell now. The boys had gone to Flanders in '14 and not come back. The girls had gone to London and stayed. Their parents ... they had gone into the churchyard, and weren't coming out until the end of days. Would Grinsfield be a forgotten name soon, one of the villages that once was, like those fallen into the sea, or abandoned in the middle ages for who knew what reason? Would motorcars fill up the empty cottages with holiday-makers from London, flash and noisy with braying gramophones and American cocktails, all desperate gaiety, like revellers who know that the last call bell will soon be rung? It was like the wake of an era, these last twenty years. Only, when would it end, and the new era begin? These Nazis in Germany ... were they the pneumonia bacillus that would carry off the old world — the old man's friend — or were they the plague that would take his children and grandchildren too?

Drewitt had been young — too young — when the parish had been given into his care. It had seemed too quiet then, too remote. Now it suited. It was a place of memories, not hope. For the country roundabout it was not so plentifully supplied with life as it once had been, if motorists were excepted. Apart from them, little in the way of life had changed since the first edition of the guide. There was talk of new industry, sometimes, that came to nothing. Even the sole new curiosity was an old one, the old confessional, the ancient black box — now disused — while a new, simpler one made by a parishioner filled its function. In their weekly ritual, the young priest entered it as the first penitent.

In the little priest's-cell, Father Drewitt sat across the grill from Stapleton, listening to the kneeling priest's recitation of his weekly weaknesses. His thoughts about a village girl. His moments of laziness, and impatience. His covetousness for a racing bicycle.

Is this what my sins were before ... before it happened? Peccadilloes? Drewitt had to restrain himself from bitter laughter. It was as if a child were confessing to Crippen, or Jack the Ripper. What if things had been different? Would there have even been a war? Would it have ended, that December in '14? Would there be Germans soldiers now in Vienna? In Czechoslovakia? Where next?

An awkward silence brought Drewitt back to simple sins. He

didn't remember most of them. A simple penance would suffice. "Say the *Oratio Dominica* and the *Ave Maria*, my son."

The confessional creaked as the two priests got to their feet to switch places. Stapleton took the priest's place. Drewitt lingered, eyeing the other, more ancient confessional that lay idle nearby, dark with age, like an old walnut wardrobe.

"Father?" prompted Stapleton.

I can't ... bear it any longer, thought Drewitt. *Looking at that thing. Every day.*

"Did you ever wonder, Father Stapleton, why there are two confessionals?"

The young priest opened his hands in submission to the mystery. "The Church has many traditions, Father. Many relics, and historical curiosities, gathered over the centuries. Perhaps a parishioner crafted a new one as an act of devotion? Or the old one is worn out but venerable with age?"

Perhaps now is the moment. Now, after all these years. To confess. Father Drewitt pulled his gaze away from the old confessional, letting his eyes drift from it to the pews, and the altar, drinking in the little church that had been a home for so long, like a man on the scaffold taking a last draught of the world before the end.

"We shall use the old one today," he told Stapleton. "Then ... then you will understand."

Drewitt opened the confessional, for the first time since that spring twenty-four years before. The wood crumbled where he touched it, like something ancient; like the artefacts excavated from Herculaneum. The other priest had already installed himself in the adjacent chamber while Drewitt stood on the threshold of the penitent's side. He stepped inside, shut himself into the dark, and knelt before the grill.

It smelt decayed, too. Not in the way of wood in the forest, softening gently over time into mould. Dry. Desiccated. Something left in a tomb since the dawn of time.

"Dawn," muttered Drewitt.

"Father?"

"The sin I must confess to you today. It is from many years ago. Before the War." *Almost before you were born.* "It was at dawn that day that the story begins. Or a little before dawn. There were birds. Grey light. I was getting dressed, in my cottage, across the road, when I heard a growling outside. The birds fell silent, and the growling came closer, down the road. Two fiery lights came around the bend there. The driver slowed, pulling in to the lane by the church."

"Oh," said Stapleton. "A motorcar."

"It was a rare sight to see a motor in Grinsfield, then. I hurried to finish dressing, not knowing what the visitor betokened. A traveller, lost? Someone official? The last rites needed in some wealthy house?

"Good morning," said the motorist heartily. He was still seated in his silver vehicle, stripped of his hat and goggles, now. He was in middle age, handsome, with the calm confidence that comes from never having known poverty, or uncertainty. Climbing out of the open-topped motorcar, he gave Drewitt's hand a vigorous shake, never taking his eyes off the priest. Blue eyes, pale like a winter sky. Smartly attired in a grey travelling suit — of a fineness that Drewitt had only ever seen distantly hinted at by the suits of the local gentry — his guest wore a silk cravat with a diamond pin.

"It blazed when the dawn light struck it," Drewitt told the other priest. "Like the morning star." *And did they not say that diamonds were made of cinders?*

Across the grill, Stapleton licked his lips. "If temptation overcame you, my son, and you took the jewel …"

Drewitt shook his head. "There is more. Let me go on."

"A fine motor, don't you think, Father?" asked the man. Probably rhetorically. He seemed as proud as Punch of it.

"Drewitt. Father Drewitt."

"Good to meet you, Father Drewitt," said the man. He had gone 'round the engine to extinguish the carbide headlamps. They were already dimming as the sun rose. "Yospher. Rex Yospher's my name."

"There was no wireless in those days," Drewitt reminded the young Stapleton. "No talkies in the picture houses. We didn't hear voices from around the world every day, so I didn't know what to make of Yospher. He dressed the way foreign princes, or Americans did, in the papers. I couldn't place him. He explained he was from Canada.

"Visiting the Mother Country, Father," said Yospher. "I have a factory that needs to be built and I am here looking for a site. Maybe in Kent. Maybe Sussex."

"Ah," said Drewitt. He was still mesmerized by the motorcar, having never had the opportunity of inspecting one at close quarters before.

Yospher smiled. "Rolls-Royce 40/50, Father. A swell piece of British engineering, if ever there was one. Rides smooth as glass. Has power in her, though. Take a seat. Try her on for size," invited Yospher, opening the door.

"Oh, I …"

"Go on. No harm in sitting in a motor, is there?"

Drewitt carefully stepped up on the running-board, and slid into the leather seat. He took in the controls with a mix of admiration and bewilderment.

"Just put your hands on the wheel," said Yospher. "Picture yourself flying down the sunken lanes, fifty horses at your beck and call with the twitch of a foot."

And Drewitt could. As if in a dream, he seemed to see the downs rolling past him as he drove, drunk with speed and unlimited power. In such a motor, he could go anywhere, free as a bird. Free as a lord, every eye swivelling towards him like compass needles as he raced past, leaving in his wake admiring men and women. *And women …*

"Cigarette?" asked Yospher. Drewitt blinked, and found a golden cigarette case open before him.

"No, thank you, I don't …"

"I'd be honoured, Father, if you'd consent to have a friendly smoke with me. They're top grade. Have them made special, by the best firm in London. Those ones on the left are Balkan Sobranie. On the right, Virginia."

"Father," scolded Stapleton, losing track, in his disapproval, of who was the penitent, "smoking during the sacrament of penitence…"

It surprised Drewitt to find that he had a lit cigarette in his hand. He continued smoking despite the young priest's pursed lips.

"Yes. I'd forgotten that it was he who gave me my first taste of tobacco. I took one, of course. Virginia. They were all stamped with a golden 'Y'. I remember being impressed by that. Only later did I ask myself what kind of man put his initial on his cigarettes."

A vainglorious one.

As they smoked in the pleasant spring dawn, Drewitt pondered again what had brought a well-heeled traveller to this corner of the county at such an hour.

"I wonder if you might show me around your church, Father," said Yospher.

An eccentric architecture-lover, Drewitt had thought. An early riser, too.

"Of course," said Yospher, seeing Drewitt thinking, "I understand there to be a fee for the privilege." Yospher found three half-sovereigns in his pocket, and passed them to the priest.

"My son, one is far too much. I do not even know if I can change *one.*"

"Consider it a donation," said Yospher. "I won't go hungry for the want of thirty shillings."

So Drewitt led his guest around the little churchyard to see a few noteworthy stones, and pointed out the features that could be read about in more detail in the sixpenny leaflet, or the county guide, while trying the Sobranie this time. Yospher expressed mild interest at all the sights, from the pointed arches to the stained glass. He was momentarily taken aback by the large crucifix, studying it for a long while before nodding and looking thoughtfully at the flagstone floor.

"I am afraid that about does it," Drewitt told his visitor. He didn't resent those who brought historical curiosity to the church, even those who did so against the spirit of the Oath Against Modernism that his Holiness, Pius X, had required of the clergy. Truth be known, Drewitt chaffed at that oath, and thought modernism to be not *all* bad.

"There's one other thing, Father," said Yospher. "The thing is, well, I've never been a religious man. But for some time now I've felt … I guess you could say a need for confession. For forgiveness. It's been a long road. A long struggle. Mistakes were made.

There are things I need to get off my conscience. To move on. To start fresh. You understand, Father."

"Yes. Yes, of course, my son. If that is what you wish. Shall we go to the confessional?"

"*This* confessional?" asked Stapleton, unnecessarily, as there had been no other then.

"Yes. I sat where you do today. He was here, where I am. And the things he told me ..."

"Father!" said Stapleton, "Stop! It is a sin — worse, a sacrilege — to repeat anything, anything said under the seal of confession."

"Do you think I don't know that?" Drewitt lit another cigarette. He needed a lungful of it before continuing. "It is not *his* sin I am confessing. It is mine." What passed between him and Yospher in the confessional he would take to his grave. But he remembered. Remembered as though it were happening again before his eyes.

"Tell me what has been troubling you, my son," Drewitt said.

Yospher sighed, a sound that came through the grill like the feeling of a nation in mourning. "For a long time now, a long, long time, I've been estranged from my father."

"And you wish for a reconciliation," said the priest.

"That's about the size of it, yes."

"I don't wish to turn you away, my son, but surely it is your father you should approach. I can offer forgiveness if you have sinned against him, but it is he who must ..."

Yospher leant closer to the grill that separated them. "I *am* approaching Him, Father."

Drewitt understood now. "You mean, you are estranged from God."

"That's it, Father. That's why I've come to you."

"And in what way have you sinned against Him?"

"You name it, Father. If there was a way to vex Him, I took it."

"What, specifically, have you done, my son?"

Yospher considered, looking to the ceiling of the confessional. "I helped you find what was already inside you."

"In me?" wondered Drewitt.

"In all of you. Man. Your pride. Your hatred of each other. Your petty desires. Your weakness."

"But, why would you do that?"

"Because He thought so highly of you. Of something so … *inferior*. That was always His way. Remember how He treated Cain. Would Cain have acted as he did had he not been rejected by his Father for a younger son? Had he not been treated with contempt?"

"Do you see yourself as having been forsaken by God?"

"What would you call being cast down into Hell for eternity? All for refusing to bow to *you*."

Drewitt edged back from the grill. In a place like Grinsfield, one never encounted the elaborately mad. "Whatever you have done, my son," he said, "it cannot have been so wicked as to place you on a level with Satan himself."

"You don't understand," said Yospher contemptuously. "How could you?"

Then Drewitt saw — felt — the light drain away from the confessional, and with it the warmth, until only a suffocating black void remained which seemed to suck the very breath from his body. And not only air, but life. Hope. He gasped for air, clawing in desperation at his throat and collar as the strength bled out of his limbs. All that remained in the confessional were two pale blue eyes in the dark vacuum, eyes that watched him without sympathy as he thrashed like a drowning cat. Drewitt fell to his knees then, pressed to the floor as if a boot-heel were grinding out his life against a cold, unyielding anvil.

"Now," said Yospher, "do you know me?"

Choking, Drewitt had no breath to speak. He was dying, he was certain. He couldn't think. In his mind, he began to say the *Oratio Dominica*. And the pressure eased just enough to let him draw in a little air.

"Yes," he wheezed. "I … know you."

The pressure faded, and the confessional returned to being merely a dim, cool box.

"Why?" asked the priest. "Why have you come? Here?"

"Here? Why not here. You each take His place in the confessional, do you not?"

"Yes, but … But I cannot forgive *evil itself*."

"I am not an abstraction, Father. I am here," said Yospher. "I have come. On my knees. I want … I *ask*, forgiveness. From *you*."

"He could not have told me each of his sins," Drewitt told Stapleton. "There were not enough moments in a lifetime for their hearing. But it didn't matter. He asked forgiveness, and he must have been sincere. Nothing else would ever have bent those knees before another. I refused him."

"Why?"

"He was the Enemy. How could he be forgiven? By me, a simple priest of a village no-one has ever heard of or cared about?"

"The enemy?" asked Stapleton. "You mean, German?"

"No, of course not. This was before the War."

"Then I don't …"

"He was the Adversary, Father. The Enemy. The Fallen One."

"Father Drewitt, surely …"

"Do you believe he exists?"

"Of course, but …"

"Well. He came to me. He asked for forgiveness in His name. And I denied it, God help me. Do you understand what that means? There might have been reconciliation. The rift might have been mended, healed. The world restored. Peace with honour," said Drewitt, and laughed bitterly. "I chose not to allow it."

"Father," said Stapleton. For the first time, Drewitt saw the other priest at a loss for words.

"*That* is my sin," said Drewitt. "That is my confession. I ask forgiveness."

Stapleton sat in silence. Finally he spoke. "Father, how can I judge you for such a thing?"

Drewitt looked up at the young priest through the grill. "Will you deny forgiveness too?"

"That is not the problem. What penance could I possibly propose for such a thing? I believe your remorse, of course, but …"

"Only a few weeks later, a chain of events began which led to war," said Drewitt. "I don't see how the two events could have been connected, but I know they must have been. It was a war that ended without forgiveness. And now another is coming. There is a difference, I think, between fighting a just war, and refusing to accept the enemy's surrender. I refused."

"You can't think that the Great War was because of you, Father," said Stapleton.

"Will you allow me to choose my own penance?" asked Drewitt.

"Yes," said Stapleton, seeming relieved to have that burden lifted from his shoulders.

Peace was different things at different times. Roberts said that now it was "freedom stripped and cast to the loud pack". Another poet had once said, "The devil take order now! I'll to the throng/ Let life be short; else shame will be too long."

"Very well," said Drewitt. "To every thing there is a season. I've always been wrong with my seasons, but now, I think, I know what to do in this one." He plucked the white poppy from his coat, and pushed it through the grill to Stapleton. "My penance will be that I go back to the army, if they'll have me. A war is coming. Perhaps it's the same war, never ended. They will need priests."

Stapleton took the poppy. "I thought you believed in peace, Father."

Which was worse, the naïveté that made the young shun war at any cost, or the naïveté that made them embrace war at any cost?

"I did," said Drewitt. "At all the wrong times."

Father Drewitt rose, knees creaking, from the kneeler, and left the confessional. When Stapleton emerged, his face a mix of awe, disapproval, and confusion, the older priest handed him his packet of Woodbines.

"I'm giving up these as well," he said, and shut the door of the confessional. It broke, and crumbled to dust.

Part II

E ACH OF OUR middle trio of stories takes place largely or entirely outside the premises of the club, and all directly involve the founder, Dr Rafe Maddox who, like Shakespeare's poet, had a habit of rolling his eye from heaven to earth and then giving airy nothing a local habitation, the main difference between Maddox and a poet being the former's tendency to use a whacking great machine to accomplish the feat instead of a feather.

We go first to the London of 1869 in "The Mudmen of Tower Tunnel". For the convenience of those unfamiliar with the languages concerned, I have rendered all speech in English apart from a few obvious Latin terms. For a full transcript of these events in the original tongues, readers are invited to seek out Dr Rafe Maddox's excellent monograph "Terraform Entities from Classical to Modern Times" in Vol. 3, Series ii of *The Proceedings of the Etheric Explorers Club*. Now merely a conduit for piping, the site of this incident — Tower Subway — is unfortunately no longer accessible to the public, though the entrance kiosks may be seen at the terminal points of the subway on either side of the Thames (the more attractive round brick entrance at the Tower Hill end is not original, having been built in 1926).

The next story carries us some distance, to remote Sable Island, a vast sand bar at the edge of the continental shelf of North America — and to the 1870s. Readers familiar with the novel *Knights of the Sea*, which concerned an artefact known as the Rawlins Engine (in addition to a eugenicist conspiracy, an argentine addiction, and a werebeastie tutor), will recall that in that novel Dr Maddox alluded to his earlier visit to Nova Scotia and Sable Island, telling Elliott Graven that "Arrogance, and loss, and desperation led me there. And nearly led to, well, something rather unfortunate." In "A Visit from Prospero", we have the full details of the occasion to which he referred, involving a machine of Maddox's devising which is, regrettably, no longer in existence (unless some part of it still lies — together with the skeletons of so many grim wrecks and their passengers — beneath the ever-shifting sands of that isle).

Maddox and Brenna are together in London again two decades later, when the ancient manuscript known as *Cotton Avicenna B. iv.* draws them both into the horrible mystery which was at that time gripping the minds of London and the world. Antiquarians will recognize the manuscript's name as placing it within the famed Cottonian Library founded by Sir Robert Cotton, the *Avicenna* section of the collection being the documents of Persian and Arabic origin, whose history diverged from the rest of the library prior to the tragic Ashburnham House fire of 1731. I have spent considerable time combing the archives of the club for the glass plates upon which the manuscript was photographed by Dr Maddox in the 1880s, without finding any trace of them. Perhaps I should be thankful for the failure.

The Mud Men of Tower Tunnel

IT IS A strange fact, is it not, that a man may, after his death, be rendered into a mere few unremarkable pounds of ash and vapour? But then, they do say that man was first shaped from clay. As an engineer of mines in my native Wales, it has been my custom to think upon the dust more often than the spirit, and yet one may uncover a wonder or two if one delves deep enough beneath the earth; in the drops of golden amber dripped from an ancient bough, or in the forest itself, crushed to seams of black coal by the burden of time.

Even if he is ignorant of the ineffable, the engineer knows of the grain of grit that may seize up a fine machine. How much more delicate the human machine is! And how surpassing mysterious. It was my engineering profession that brought me to London on a grey November in 1869, for the Tower Tunnel was then nearing completion. I craved the chance to witness that lately perfected product of the science of subterranean construction, the tunnelling shield of Barlow and Greathead. With it, they had promised to accomplish in a year what had taken Marc Brunel nearly twenty: to span the Thames from below, and moreover, establish the first underground tube railway. Oh, there were greater undertakings in the world, to be sure. Why, only the previous week the mighty had celebrated, in Egypt, the great canal. A wonder, there is no doubt. But mining is in my blood, and I would sooner creep a mile through the earth, bent double, than float down any number of canals in luxury.

To my slight annoyance I found, upon my arrival at the offices of Mr James Henry Greathead, that he had failed make himself available at the appointed hour. Out of fairness to him, I re-examined the letter in which he had assented to my visit, confirming my punctuality and his inexplicable tardiness. It may have crossed my mind at that moment that Greathead was, after all, but twenty-five. A mere crot of a boy to be in command of such an enterprise. His staff, it seemed, knew no more than I his whereabouts, but one suggested that I should seek him out at the tunnelling site, for Greathead was wont to inspect the progress at odd hours. I thanked the clerk and, there being no Hansoms about, proceeded by growler to the Tower of London.

The added expense of the four-wheeler, compounding as it did my irritation at the cab's foetid interior, put me in no good state of mind upon my arrival at the tunnel-head off Lower Thames Street, with the Tower of London looming menacingly over the work site. It reminded one of the antiquity of the spot, home to such a menagerie over the ages, from centurions, to beheaded traitors, to Blake's tyger. Immediately, the inactivity of the scene impressed itself upon me; in the normal course of a dig such as the Tower Tunnel, a continual flux of persons and earth is to be expected. But here the carts were still, and no workmen busied themselves with the hundred tasks of a normal day. Instead, when the cabman had made my change, I found myself greeted only by a specimen of that style of idle, brash male which the metropolis evidently creates through some form of foul spontaneous generation, just as the Thames once issued forth noxious vapours, to the detriment of all who huddled about her banks. But then, as my countryman Alfred Russel Wallace said, "We constantly find details of the marvellous adaptation of animals to the localities in which they are found."

This slovenly fellow, in his chequered lounge suit and bowler hat, leant against the pit-head with casual effrontery, rolling a cigar about his lips. I could see, of course, that he was of the sort who live by crime, or betting, or on the proceeds of some unnatural vice, such as journalism. Making out the black-lead tucked behind his right ear, I divined that it was in this latter class that he belonged, since the place was an unlikely haunt for a bookie.

"'Ere about the mudmen, would you be, sir?"

At first I failed to take the rascal's meaning, but grasped belatedly that he was using some local cant to refer to the excavators.

"The *mudmen* appear to be having a half-holiday today," I observed. The fellow scratched his head at this; however I have often observed that Cockneys have difficulty understanding the Welsh

accent. Rather than bandy any further words with fools, I strode
into the pithead lift and, shutting the cage, pulled the lever for
descent. The lift juddered a trifle before it settled into a steady
slow decline, exchanging thin daylight and its bewildered repor-
ters for the snug, lamp-lit depths. As I fell, it struck me how like
the surface world is to the insubstantial watercolours in which its
landscapes are so often depicted. Pale, bloodless, almost illusory.
So unlike the depths, with their blackness as deep as any sea. A
pool of golden light brought below only makes the endless night
seem the darker. It is a world for Dutch Masters, for oils; black,
thick, and solid.

Judging the lift's height at nearly twelve feet, I would say the
shaft was sixty from top to bottom. Perhaps as far below London
as anyone has ever gone. The air took on a damp, rivery smell as
the lift descended. It was the scent of wet mud, rather than stone,
but the two are like enough to be kin. No doubt the same silt that
boatmen know extends downward scores of feet, through centuries
of tides, to the ancient bedrock of England. But no sooner had my
musings gotten into their stride than the lift clattered to rest in the
tunnel itself, at the mouth of a cylindrical tube only seven feet or
so in diameter. Along its length gas jets at waist-height were burning regularly every four or five paces. They flickered in the draught
revealing, in their shifting light, a pair of figures approaching.

"Smith!" One of them shouted, his voice strangely shrill in the
metal walls of the tunnel. "Is that you Smith? Blast you, I told you
to keep out of here!" As they neared, plodding over the mucky
floor of the tunnel in huge Wellington boots, topped with oversized
Mackintoshes, I found familiar features in the face that was looking daggers at me.

"No smiths here, sir. Only a Welsh miner."

Greathead missed a beat in his stride as his face went from fury
to astonishment. "Folland! It's you! I thought it was that accursèd
so-called journalist coming down to pester us again."

They drew even with the lift gate and I made out the other
gentleman's features for the first time. He was similarly attired
to Greathead, and of a like age, but with the dark hair of the Celt,
though having something of the Mediterranean about his nose
as well, I thought. He looked ill at ease, his hands gripping too

tightly on an ebony walking stick, and his eye always straying to the glistening iron ribs of the tunnel, as if he felt oppressed by the immense mass of earth and river above. It is a state often seen in those unused to the underground.

"But Folland," Greathead continued, a little out of breath, "what the devil brings you down here?"

I smiled ruefully at young Greathead. "Why, I only wrote a month ago to say I was coming." Shaking my head, I could hardly help but notice the state of him. "You're in full fuss about something, and no mistake. Is it these mudmen, causing you troubles?"

Greathead seemed to fairly start out of his Wellingtons at the mention of mudmen.

"Why? What do you know of them?" he asked, more agitated than ever.

"Nothing, my lad, nothing. Only that rascal up there said they were giving you the gyp."

"Oh. Well, I would value your advice, God knows. Get yourself a Mac and Wellies," he suggested, waving to the closet behind the lift shaft. "This is Doctor Rafe Maddox, by the way," he said, finally introducing the other gentlemen. "Doctor Maddox, Renfrew Folland, mining engineer."

Perhaps remembering at last why I had come, Greathead led us back down the long, ribbed, cast iron tube, telling me of its construction in an abstracted manner, his mind wandering elsewhere.

"Funny, isn't it," I commented, "to think that at this very moment wherries and steamers are passing over our heads. Almost like being under one of the canal viaducts when a barge is going by."

Maddox nodded, nervously, but failed to see the humour in the thing.

"We've been averaging five feet per day, with good days going up to nine feet. As you can see," Greathead continued, pointing out the piping that ran the length of the tunnel, "we use hydraulic pressure to drive the shield forward through the mud, removing earth as we go and re-enforcing the tunnel with sections of iron tubing."

"You must get some seepage," I said, noting the slurry of mud we walked through.

"Not so much as you would imagine. The tube is sealed with

grout. There are no less than twenty-two feet of clay above the tunnel at any point."

After about a thousand feet we came to the workface, where the circular tunnelling shield marked the furthest point of excavation. Much of the shield was taken up by a huge iron door that gave access to the clay, which was hacked away and shovelled though the portal by the workmen, as testified by a great heap of mud at the opening. All around it, the tube was littered with the workers' equipage, carelessly discarded in the dirt as though tossed away in an emergency. Mandrels and spades lay jumbled with cloth caps and water-jacks, and tommy boxes thrown amongst them, some fallen open with untouched lunches tumbled out and spoilt.

"Appears your mudmen left in a bit of a rush," I observed.

"What? What do you mean?" Greathead asked, genuinely baffled.

"Ah," said Doctor Maddox, "I think there may be a misunderstanding. You see," he continued, addressing me now, "by *mudmen* we are referring not to the workers who shovel mud here. Rather, it is the term used by the excavators to describe the huge, shambling creatures of mud which attacked them." Greathead gave several tense nods of assent to this clarification.

"Creatures!" I exclaimed, "What creatures are these? Do you mean to tell me there's something living down here?"

Greathead threw up his hands in despair. "That's what they all say. None of them will return to work. They believe this, this *thing* will do them in. What's worse, they're spreading the tale amongst their colleagues. I doubt there's a digger left in the Home Counties who'd consent come down here now."

I had heard many queer tales from miners through the years, and not a few wild inventions, but never so brazen a piece of foolishness as that to which I was now listening.

"Surely you don't credit this nonsense, Greathead! It's a ploy, for higher wages, or some such thing. Attacked by mudmen, honestly! I blame sensational literature. These serials in the papers, they excite the weak-minded."

"To be strictly accurate," Doctor Maddox interjected, "only one such creature has ever been witnessed." A drip was wetting Maddox's forelock, and he cast a worried look up at the source

— an iron seam that wanted more grout — before stepping out of the path of the water. "Assuming that the same being is appearing in each case." Maddox examined the ceiling of the tube again with suspicion. "You *are* certain this tunnel is stable, Greathead? I understand that Brunel's suffered a cave-in when…"

"Doctor Maddox," I interrupted, still flabbergasted by the whole notion, "you don't mean to suggest that you give credence to this idiocy. Surely as a man of medicine it would behove you to look upon this as a manifestation of madness." I sniffed and squinted at one of the gas jets that bubbled away in its nook in the tubing. "Or some influence in the atmosphere. Gas, from the lights or trapped in the mud?"

Greathead stirred from his funk. "Doctor Maddox is not a physician, you understand, but a scientist with a … a curiosity for the mysterious. He has been kind enough to offer his assistance in this inexplicable business."

Maddox passed me a card inscribed with his name, and below it, *The Etheric Explorers Club, St. Raphael's Square, London.*

"Etheric?" I asked. "As in the luminiferous ether?"

"In a sense. We're interested in non-material phenomena. The spirit, for instance."

"This farcical boggin, or mud-beast, or whatever it is, doesn't sound very spiritual to me."

"In the experience of our society, the material level of existence is often entangled with the spirit level, giving rise to a variety of unusual phenomena."

I confess I smirked a little wryly then at Greathead, as I patted my coat pocket. "Indeed, sir, I always keep a spirit level close at hand — to measure the tunnel gradients."

Greathead smiled weakly at my joke, but remained in a black mood, perhaps sensing the doom of his first great work should the digging not return to schedule. However, I could not see that his conundrum would be helped by charlatans and mumbo-jumbo.

Maddox, still showing nervousness at the river water percolating through the tubing, persisted in his purpose. "Surely," he said, "you acknowledge the existence of more than the ponderable matter of everyday life?"

I waved a dismissive hand. "Oh, I know some of these philosophers, and the fakirs out east, say the world is all imagination. Or else they claim it's nothing but spirit, and vapour, and fluff, and who knows what else. But get one of them down the mine, with a thousand ton of stone hanging over his head and he'll change his tune."

Whether either of my companions were willing to concede the point, I was not to know, for they both stayed lost in their own thoughts: Maddox, prodding with his stick the scattering of articles on the mud-heap, perhaps searching for some after-glow of the spirit realm; Greathead kneading his chin with a distracted air, like a man wondering where he had mislaid his beard. I decided I would have none of it.

"I've travelled all the way from blessèd Wales to have a look at your tunnelling machine, Greathead! I do think you might show me something of it!"

As I'd hoped, this challenge drew Greathead out of his black mood, at least for a short spell. With growing passion, he told me of the advantages of his tunnelling shield over past designs, of the stresses the iron ribbing could bear, and of the prodigious engines that drove the hydraulics. Truly, I could find no fault in his plans and machines. The only weak stone in the structure, sadly, was the keystone: the men at the work-face. No amount of steam power nor ironmongery would finish the tunnel without diggers in the shield to shovel away the earth. I said as much to Greathead, regretting the words at once, for they cast him back into the gloom of defeat.

"Come," I said, as heartily as I could, "let's have a look at the business-end of this tube of yours." I beckoned Greathead through the square orifice in the giant metal disc of the tunnelling shield, and then invited Doctor Maddox to follow him.

"If you're finished examining the diggers' rubbish," I added.

"That's quite all right, I'll remain out here if it's all the same to you."

"Damn it, man, you're not afraid of a little mud, are you?" With rising impatience, I herded Maddox, resisting, through the tunnelling shield and into the narrow gap between it and the oozing wall of mud still to be excavated. Swinging my own leg through the opening, I paused, trying to work some bend into the other knee, stiffened by a rock-fall years previous.

"Really, Doctor Maddox! I expected a little more fortitude of a man who makes it his business to chase down ghouls."

As I sat astride the opening, there was a sharp intake of breath from within the dark gap.

"Have you stubbed your toe, Doctor?" I inquired.

"God Almighty," muttered Greathead.

A shadow startled me, and a strange heavy presence. I half turned to see what it was. Someone was there, just behind me, standing atop the heap of clay left from the last shift of digging. But not someone. A shapeless, faceless pillar, like a grey half-melted waxwork, loomed over me, an arms-length away. On one side, something began to separate from the pillar. A limb. An arm. The stump extended toward me. Before I could say or do anything, hands seized me from behind and dragged me backward through the portal. It slammed shut with a clang, plunging me in the most profound darkness.

A match flared; Greathead lit a gas jet to brighten the thin crack we were crammed into, just ahead of the shield face. The tremor of his hand danced the match flame wildly about until he tossed it away into the muck. Such was the narrowness of the gap we occupied, that as I scrambled to my feet I found I was blundering into both the steel tunnelling shield in front and the wall of oozing mud behind.

Maddox's breathing was sounding stertorous, and his eyes looked a trifle bulging in the stark light of the gas, but he was the first to shake off the shock.

"There's something in this after all, it seems," he said, between shallow breaths.

Straightening my Mac, I turned with some little difficulty to face him.

"We've all had a little scare," I said, laughing, "but it's obvious now what's been happening, isn't it?" I glanced at Greathead, who was gawping blankly at the iron wall in front of his nose, showing no signs of assent. "It's a prank. One of Greathead's competitors would like to scare him off and make a fool of him. Mark my words. It's some fellow caked in mud. Probably sneaked in after the last shift. One of the workmen, paid off to scuttle the project.

Mudmen! Ha!"

My only answer came in the form of a great thud that shook the tunnelling shield, sending us jumping by reflex into the mud wall behind us. Another thud, and the drumming became regular, almost furious. Greathead had jammed himself into the corner to my right, while Maddox was gasping raggedly, though the air was still relatively good. It wouldn't long remain so, sealed into the gap with two other men and a gas flame.

"Cheeky devil. Plays the part well, I'll give him that. But we can't stay in here forever. Doctor Maddox, please be so kind as to hand me that stick of yours."

Maddox nodded enthusiastically at the notion of escape – he really seemed to me a most easily excitable young man – and he passed me his cane. With a heave, I shifted the iron door aside. At once, the rascal without ceased his pummelling of the shield and stood still, staring I would have said, had I been able to see his eyes through the clay. The others peered around the opening to have a look for themselves at the pest. Suspecting that the layer of mud would cushion any thrashings I gave the fellow, I grasped the cane like an épée and leant out to thrust it as forcefully as I could into his belly. Little did I imagine how literally I would succeed. The stick penetrated the outer layer of clay, as I expected. It continued, passing straight through his middle until a mere six inches stuck out. Thinking I had somehow killed the knave, I released the stick and lurched back, smacking my head on the edge of the doorway as I did. But he showed no sign of distress. Indeed, he drew out the stick that was impaling him as casually as one might pull out a wallet. I slammed the door shut again, dumbfounded. It had gone right through. There was no… no body inside.

"What… what on God's earth is it, Maddox?" Greathead exclaimed, accompanied by the renewed beating of the mudman on our narrow fortress.

Doctor Maddox had closed his eyes, perhaps for better concentration or to settle his mind. He was still respiring heavily.

"A golem, possibly. A number of rabbis, starting with Elijah of Chelm, were reputed to have animated creatures from clay. What if one had been created, and then lost in the Thames? Or disposed of there. Gad, might it even have walked here on the sea bed before sinking into the river mud? If one were made, but the Word never removed from its head... do either of you know Hebrew?"

I looked incredulously at Greathead, and then back at Maddox. "Of course we don't know Hebrew. We're engineers, not bloody rabbis!" I said. Even I was beginning to find the cramped space unnerving, particularly as the creature on the other side was scrabbling now at the steel, screeching like nails across a slate. "What bloody good are you, Maddox? I thought you were meant to be a dab hand at these things."

"Please try to understand, Mr Folland," he said, massaging his temples as he did, "that *I* have never encountered a golem either. I don't suppose anyone has, not for seventy years, since the Sabbath Conflagration at Drohiczyn, back during the wars with the French."

Greathead looked past me to Maddox. "What exactly do you propose that we do?"

"Firstly, extricate ourselves from this crevice."

While I was cocking nose at this inspired suggestion, Maddox continued.

"It seems to me that we then have two choices," he said, pausing a moment to shudder at an especially shrill scratching on the shield, "we may either push our way past and flee towards the lift..."

"A great idea," I interrupted, "by all means."

"...or, we may choose to subdue the golem, by extracting the Shem, or name of God, written on a tablet in its mouth. I should tell you there may be a certain amount of danger in this latter course."

I snorted. "If you imagine that I am going to put my hand in the mouth of that, that, golem, and rummage about for tablets, then you're a more imaginative man than myself, Doctor Maddox!"

I turned to Greathead for support, but he was already looking past me again, his face furrowed with worry.

"And if we do not stop it, Maddox, what then?"

The self-styled Etheric Explorer finally opened his eyes to return Greathead's gaze. "It may well run amok," he said, before the thing's scratching changed back into an echoing pounding again. "Continue to run amok, I should say. We can have no way of knowing what its objective is. It could well destroy the tunnel."

Greathead groaned. "We must stop it, Maddox. Whatever you need of me, just say the word."

"Very well. You needn't worry on account of your hands, Mr Folland," Maddox said, pulling on a pair of kid gloves that looked a poor sort of gauntlet for the undertaking, "I shall attempt to extricate the Shem. You and Greathead must try to pinion the golem's arms in order to afford me the opportunity. Are you game for it?"

"Damn it, man, it's not me who needs to get his gummel up. You don't imagine I'll stand by and watch as poor Greathead's tube gets smashed up by that abomination!"

Maddox nodded and bade me open the hatch, whereupon he sprang out with an eagerness I would hardly have credited had I not witnessed it. He deftly dove past the creature, nearly crashing into the tunnel wall in the process, and jumped about behind the golem to distract the thing whilst Greathead and I exited through the tunnelling shield. The ruse worked; the thing turned its faceless clay bulk toward his capering and hand-waving, allowing us a few seconds to slip into the tunnel and fall upon it from behind, each taking hold of one of the awful, doughy clay arms. The thing twisted to free itself without effect. Maddox approached, stretching a hand for the thing's mouth. Beside me, Greathead was pale as death, so I turned a cheering smirk of triumph on him.

It was at that moment that matters whirled out of control. It is often the way, isn't it? One moment you can be strolling down a mine shaft, humming a tune, all thoughts of trouble banished, and the next a gas-pocket ignites, sucking the air from your lungs, or a rock fall entombs you for eternity. Regaining its senses, or its strength, the creature lifted Greathead and me aloft like children, except that the tunnel was too low and we were dashed against the ceiling before it hurled us down so roughly that I hardly knew what was happening. First I was upside down, gravity all topsy-turvy, the next instant the earth knocked the wind out of me and I slithered down the slight incline of the mud heap and into Greathead's motionless body, jumbled like a rag doll, with blood trickling past his eye. Dimly, for my brain was sluggish after being knocked about, I perceived that Maddox, too, had been thrown some distance toward the lift end of the tunnel. It seemed to stretch away to infinity. For the first time, I began to wish myself out of the earth, back in the sane open air, where the cabbies and bankers, lords and paupers, were even at that moment going about their banal business, blind to the horrors beneath their feet.

Dazed as I was, I could see we had but one opportunity to save ourselves before the colossus beat our skulls to mince against the iron walls. The stout creature was as still and blank as an unfinished statue, pointed towards Maddox's prostrate body. Shakily, I crept on hands and knees to get behind the mudman one more time. But it was too late. The head swivelled with unnatural calm in my direction. I backed away on my elbows through the mud, groping to no avail for a shovel, or mandrel, or anything that could keep the thing at bay. It advanced, and in the narrow tunnel I was easily hunted to the wall, with the monster bent over me, tilting its head this way and that as if to have a better look at me with its dull, eyeless face. It drew closer still, until the blank grey head was barely a hand span from my nose. Its huge mouth slackened, for what purpose I shuddered to think, and that was when I saw my last chance. In a wink I plunged my hand up to the knuckles between its jaws. The creature fell on me with all its bulk in a crushing embrace, but I would not extract my hand. I probed for the tablet that Maddox said animated the thing. There was nothing, just more clay. It was only when it bit me savagely that I withdrew my hand at last, bellowing a string of Welsh blasphemies I had not heard uttered for years. Had you cared to ask me at that moment, and had I the leisure to reply, I might well have claimed with some certainty that I should never hear such oaths, nor anything else, ever again, for the mud-beast had grown enraged by my assault, and was venting its spleen, if it had one, on my helpless body.

Even as I began to doubt the wisdom of leaving this life uttering foul words, the creature stayed its maul-like fist in mid swing. It lurched upright and away, working its jaw as if trying to reprimand my language. I had my mangled fingers around a spade, ready to strike the thing, when Maddox's voice echoed down the tunnel. He was up now, and approaching, cautiously.

"Wait! What did you say to it?" he said.

I pulled myself out of the muck as well, keeping the spade edge aimed at the mudman. I shook my head, partly to clear it, and to dismiss any thought of my words having affected the thing. "Just some nasty language, Doctor Maddox," I said.

"I know it's Welsh," he said, "but really, you mustn't dismiss your native tongue so easily. I'm sure it has some redeeming qualities. *The Mabinogion*, for example…" he began, rambling.

"I *mean*," I said, growing quite exasperated, "some nasty language *in Welsh*. Things I don't care to repeat in the Queen's English."

For a tense moment, Maddox looked lost in thought, as the creature turned ponderously from one of us to the other, and back. The spade was a good, sharp clay-cutting implement, and I had it level with the creature, in case it flew into a fury once again.

Maddox lifted a hand to me. "Speak to it again. In Welsh."

I shook the spade. "What do you expect me to say to the thing? 'Lovely weather we're having, considering?' 'Enjoying the tunnel?' 'Tuppence to use the lift?'"

The creature, watching our debate, was shifting from foot to foot now, agitated.

"Whatever you like," Maddox said quickly.

I struggled for an appropriate phrase.

"Listen well, you great ugly pile of foetid Thames mud. You have had your little bit of fun. Now begone, or you shall be sorry in your heart when I give you back for this," I said, holding out my bloodied fingers, "with interest!"

To underscore my point, I brandished the spade a trifle more aggressively. In response, the creature took a step closer, still jibbering silently.

"Go on," Maddox entreated. "It's reacting somehow to you. Keep it up."

Doubtful in the extreme, I maintained my harangue of the creature, offering more remarks upon its personal appearance, the propriety of its behaviour, its manifold menaces to the art of engineering, as well as chastising it for killing poor Greathead (only later did I notice that he was still breathing, and merely senseless). By the time I had truly gotten into my stride as I produced this torrent of verbal vitriol in the sonorous tongue of Wales, I had begun to detect an extraordinary influence. Not only had the monster fixed upon me with rapt attention, but it had begun to undergo a peculiar and grotesque transformation. Its amorphous, corpulent body rippled and flowed, the flesh, or clay, seeming to melt away, oozing slowly in waves and lumps towards the floor of the tunnel. It was such a disgusting spectacle that I was rendered speechless, until Maddox approached, waving for me to continue. For indeed, the creature had halted its metamorphosis, which resumed again as soon as I went back to berating it. I could hardly think of what to say next, but somehow went on blithering, mesmerized by the change. Something was emerging, as though melted from the mud by warm words. Something human, or resembling such at any rate, slowly surfaced, shedding its garment of clay. A face, a young woman's face, appeared out of the shapeless head, the horrible slash of a mouth closing up into cheeks, and lips. A fine, shapely nose was revealed, and brows, and hollows for eyes. And then the lids opened. Grey eyes, all grey, made of clay, looked back at me.

My words ran out at last. They were no longer needed in any case; the woman was fully revealed, like a new-formed Aphrodite awaiting her sculptor's kiln. Maddox, beside me now, was as speechless as I. In his case, I attribute the dumbness to being a bachelor. Out of decency, I pulled off my Mackintosh and wrapped it about the clay woman, whose mouth was now moving in a less threatening manner, as if merely trying to address us. Maddox and I waited, as some delicate anatomical adjustments were evidently yet underway. The woman, for I now thought of her as such, gasped, groaned, and wheezed in frustrated whispers. We motioned encouragingly, and presently her voice showed signs of returning. She made some sounds, and then spoke, at first muffled and indistinct. I relayed her words in English to Maddox as I made sense of them.

"Lll ...Llllet me out. Let me out," she said.

"Let you out of where? Out of here?"

"Out of thisss ... iron snake," she said, scanning her eyes over the tunnel ceiling. "You ... you two are British gods?"

This last convinced me that I was missing something of her meaning, and I explained to Maddox that the woman's dialect was unfamiliar to me.

"Gods, you say," Maddox mused. "Ask her who she is."

I relayed the question, adding that we would help her if we could.

For a long while she thought, clay brows wincing at the effort. "Bren-na." she said. "He killed me, there," she said, pointing slightly upward through the tunnel wall in the general direction of London Bridge. "Under the bridge. Should never have gone. He deserted. Thought I would betray him. Should never have gone."

In spite of everything that I had already seen, those words, 'he killed me,' set my skin to crawling. The thing was no hoax, nor a magician's weird plaything, but a real woman, dead, walking and talking.

"Let me go, let me out," she said, more urgently now, reaching for me.

"Assure her we will help," Maddox said, "but find out a little more."

Baffled as to how I might calm a ghost, I took one of her thin, cold hands and patted it, telling her we would do what we could, and asked her to tell us something of herself. In a more settled state, she tried to remember her past.

"I ... remember the fire. When the old bridge burnt. O, I should never have gone to the bridge with him," she said. From her face, I could only describe her as weeping tearlessly.

"What of you?" I said, trying to avoid the murder which so naturally preoccupied the woman's mind.

"The fire ... it was after the great one came. I was... five years old. My birth was ... the year he was crowned. He became a god on the year I was twenty-one."

"Gods, again," Maddox said. "Ask her what year she died."

It seemed ill-mannered to harp upon so troubling a subject, and I said as much to Maddox, but asked all the same. She looked overwrought, but answered.

"In the reign of Pius. The eighth year. The year after he built the great wall in the north."

Maddox started. "Pius," he repeated. "Antoninus Pius. Augustus. Pontifex Maximus."

The woman, Brenna, now twitched her gaze toward Maddox. She took hold of his Mac and said something I could not make out, but which Maddox translated for me, as I did the Welsh.

"Are you a Roman god, then? For pity, I beg you to release me! A mistake, it was a mistake! I was meant for someplace else, not this Roman underworld. Let me go! Let me go to Mag Mell at last. I am not a Roman, but I have been crawling through your underworld for... for... how long? Who is Emperor now? Still Pius?"

Maddox licked his lips and looked a little desperately in my direction. He swallowed and turned back to her, speaking in Latin. "Many years have passed, Brenna. The, ah, Pontifex Maximus in Rome has changed. He is... a different Pius. Pius Nonus. The ninth."

"Nine? So long? But you will release me? Please?"

I nearly wept myself at her anguish. To think of this poor woman, not just murdered, but left to creep alone through the muck of the Thames for seventeen centuries. It was too pitiful.

Again I soothed her, taking her hands from Maddox, whom she had been shaking alarmingly.

"We are no gods, British or Roman," I told her. "Maddox here is a ... a scholar, and I am an engineer. A builder. This is a tunnel," I said, waving at the walls, and I pointed to Greathead, unconscious, but breathing, I now saw, "built by this man. If you wish to leave the tunnel, we will show you a way out."

"Not gods?" she muttered. She sat heavily down on the floor. "You are not Roman gods? Then you cannot release me from this underworld once and for all?"

The woman despaired in silence while we looked impotently on. I could see Maddox wished to interrogate the woman more, but that her distress was restraining him. I took him aside and we conferred in undertones.

"There must be something to be done for the poor woman," I said. "Leaving her to wander as a shade, lost forever, it's too terrible. I see now that there is some reality to the matters you study, but this is no soulless golem. What do you suggest? Surely we can undo this curse somehow."

He peered over my shoulder at Brenna, so wretched and pitiable in my filthy overcoat. "Too little is known about ancient religion. Especially in Britain. Who knows what rites they used to pass the dead into the next world?"

I felt some inkling of Brenna's despair, that even Maddox, who was meant to be learned in occult matters, was flummoxed. Then it struck me, such that I actually smote the tunnel wall in shame and amazement. "Maddox, we're a pair of bloody fools! Of course! *She* knows!" I said.

We rushed to the woman and crouched before her.

"Brenna," Maddox said, "You were never buried properly, were you? Can you tell us how to do it?"

"If we perform the right funeral ritual, will that free you?" I asked, when she looked confused.

At first she said nothing, but merely stretched out her hands, trying to touch the tunnel walls. Rising, she swept her arms this way and that through the air. It appeared almost a demonstration of some hypnotic ceremonial dance. The strange face, living and yet not living, turned to us again, less terrified now.

"I forgot what it was to move. So many years in clay," she said.

"Will burial set you free?" I asked again.

Panic distorted her features again, and she backed away. "You won't put me back in the mud, not back there! Not where I belong, not where our dead go!"

Raising his hands, placatingly, Maddox lowered his voice. "Tell us how to send you to the afterlife of your people, and we will help you if we can."

In halting phrases, Brenna recollected the practices of her own time and people, struggling as much as you or I would if called upon to lay out the complete funeral service of the Church of England. The details gradually came back to her, in scattered recollections of long-forgotten hearsay, and of graveyards: the places burials could and could not take place, offerings, ritual beheadings. Macabre words to have from a dead woman, under the earth. Maddox nodded, taking note of every detail.

"Coins in the mouth, too," he said. "Interesting. A mix of Roman and indigenous rituals."

Maddox's interrogation went on for some time until, diverging onto historical tangents to satisfy his antiquarian curiosity, he bombarded the unfortunate woman with question after question on life in ancient London, whereupon I took him aside.

"See here Maddox, this isn't a lecture on classics. We know what we must do. Now let us end this poor woman's suffering, not prolong it with your idle badgering."

Though annoyed, Maddox looked to Brenna, now gazing rapturously into a bright gas jet and flicking her clay fingers in wonder through the fire. To look at her, she might have been an ordinary woman of thirty or thereabouts, if one avoided close scrutiny. To think that she had walked the earth, or beneath it, so long! It defied belief. And yet belief was forced upon me.

"Belief, then, is not voluntary. How, then, can it be meritorious?" I muttered.

Maddox raised his eyebrows.

"Something a Welshman said. Alfred Russel Wallace."

"Wallace? Flying-frog Wallace? I didn't think he was Welsh."

"Never mind that, how are we to lay the poor woman to rest, at long last?"

Instead of answering me, however, a slight smile crossed his features, and he addressed her.

"Brenna, how would you like to see the sun again, and see what your city of Londinium has become?"

"Maddox," I cautioned, taking hold of his arm and lowering my voice in spite of our English being meaningless to Brenna, "I'll not have you making a freak show of her to amuse your club!" Maddox shrugged me off and went to Brenna, who had ceased playing with the gas flame, though she still stared into it.

"The sun? I though you said you were not a god. You can take me back to the world?" she asked.

"There is a way, at the end of the tunnel."

"Maddox ..." I said again.

"London is a great city now," he continued, ignoring my objections, "larger than Rome. As ancient now as Rome was when you lived."

She peered down the tunnel, perhaps trying to imagine the metropolis that her town had become, greater than a Rome she had never seen either, in any age.

"I would like to see the sun again. And Londinium." Brenna tugged pensively at her earlobe, perhaps expecting to find some favourite bauble of contemplation there. Instead, disconcertingly, the clay lobe came away in her fingers.

"Maddox," I said, sternly, "if you mean to treat this woman as a ... a *specimen* ..."

But Maddox cut me off. "Don't be a fool! I won't entomb her

down here in this miserable tube. Even if we opened up this iron cladding and played out the ceremonies of burial, do you really imagine I would put her back into that same appalling mud that has been her prison for so many ages? You may well be at home down here, but for ordinary people," which he indicated with a quick snap of the hand from himself to Brenna, "the underworld is an unnatural place of discomfort, if not terror."

Sensing our dispute, the woman was reminded of her own doubts. "How will I reach the afterlife? Is there nothing you can do?"

"Brenna," Maddox said, stooping a little to meet her uniform grey eyes, for she was somewhat below his height, "If you should decide you have had enough of this world, I shall make you a grave, or barrow, with whatever goods and rites you ask for."

"A barrow?" she asked, "Like the old heroes and kings had?" Her clay eyes widened, dreaming of palaces of the dead. "No, it's too fancy," she concluded, before thinking better of it. "Well, if it is not too much trouble. Thank you very much."

"Don't doubt that I will hold you to that promise, Maddox," I said.

Maddox reassured me, a little huffily and ineffectually, that his family had always honoured their word, even in the days when they had been slavers and pirates. Reluctantly, I accepted his guarantees.

"But how do you propose to leave this place without being observed?"

"The journalist, you mean?"

"He's hardly likely to miss a clay woman strolling out of the lift." By now Greathead was stirring, moaning a little as he came back to consciousness. It suggested an idea to me. "What if I ascend with Greathead, and press the reporter into lending assistance. We'll take Greathead to a physician, saying he's knocked his head in an accident."

It was necessary to help Greathead to his feet. On catching sight of Brenna he gabbled a few incoherent exclamations, which I silenced as well as I could with reassurances. "The tunnel is safe. Everything is under control." I am certain he would have persisted in complaining and craning his neck about for another sight of

Brenna even as I guided him away, but for the fact his skull was evidently throbbing, to judge by the hand he steadied it with. Maddox followed us, leading Brenna to the lift. Once Greathead and I were aboard, Maddox lent a hand in dropping the gate.

"Mind what you have promised," I cautioned him.

Maddox nodded. "I shall defend Miss Brenna's privacy as assiduously as I do my own. Even more so. But do come by my club after matters quieten down a bit. We'll speak more about this."

I patted the pocket where I had lodged his card.

"You might meet Wallace there," Maddox added.

"Surely Alfred Wallace is not a member?"

"Oh, he's been attending our meetings for some time. Been a spiritualist for years."

If Wallace attended, I would have to look into the thing. I tried to think of some suitable farewell for Brenna, but found myself at a loss, hardly knowing what to make of her strange adventure, or doom, and my slight part in it. I pulled a florin from my cab change and passed it through the grill to her, my fingers still sore from her bite. "A solidus," I said. "Should you ever choose to leave this world, dear lady, I would be honoured if it should be my coin that you took on your journey."

Brenna and Maddox dropped away as the lift carried Greathead and me back up to London. I hastily instructed my fellow engineer to say nothing of mudmen, only that an accident had happened. As I expected, the reporter, Smith, was easily duped. Not at all a bad sort, as it turned out, for he hailed us a cab at once and even suggested a man in Harley Street, which was as well for the capital was not my home, and Greathead was in no condition to issue instructions.

Greathead recovered to finish his tunnel, and a good many other projects in the following decades. Whether we unwittingly offended some hoary old divinity that day, or the tunnel was simply a damn-fool idea to begin with, it of course failed soon after its celebrated unveiling the following year. Perhaps Maddox was correct, that the common man dislikes dark passages. In his own case, he later confided, his terror of tight spaces was born from an incident in his youth when two cousins had endevoured to bury him alive. Whatever the origin of men's whims, after some small success as a foot-tunnel the tube finally closed, shortly before Great-head's recent untimely death, the year the Tower Bridge spanned the Thames so majestically over top of the old tunnel.

As for Brenna, Maddox was as good as his word, showing her many of the marvels of modern Britain, and once accustomed to our world she insisted upon mixing herself up in his curious pur-suits. At last, though, a longing for the next world overcame her, and she used my florin to be ferried there, or for whatever purpose her people's rites dictate. She now journeys in that other land, her bones resting comfortably in the barrow Maddox created for her, only returning to walk this world once a twelve-month, on All Souls Day.

A Visit from Prospero

I WAS RIDING ON the dunes when the faint grey line of smoke appeared on the northern horizon. A steamer out of Halifax, but not our supply ship; that was not due for a fortnight. Certainly this ship seemed to be heading straight for us. Unexpected visitors generally came to Sable Island only in tragedy, ringing the long crescent sliver of sand with wrecks through the years. Seeing that ship, the morbid thought sprang to my mind that her crew might go blindly on until they foundered on the bar that lay just off shore, spilling out of their ship to strive desperately for land. It was a common-enough scene, but a chilling one nonetheless. Perhaps such a circumstance is best left unimagined, lest thinking should make it come to pass.

Father had arrived on the island eighteen years earlier, bringing his bride with him from the warmer sands of Egypt. His passion was to root out the secrets of ancient prophesy. The years spent in the desert monasteries and in excavating discarded scrolls of the Coptic gospels had built in him a conviction that the fall of Rome had severed the unity of our knowledge of prophesy by dividing the known world, leaving key texts outside the ken of western scholars, as Alexandria fell first from orthodoxy, and then from Christendom. The fragments that he had copied or recovered had occupied his full attention since leaving the East. Mother died soon after my birth, and so I never knew her, though I visited her grave often. In the next life, I hope that she and I will have the opportunity to become acquainted. It was for her that I was given my middle name, Violet *Aziza* Ketchum.

Seeing that the ship would take some little while to arrive, and since I was several miles west of the main station where its passengers were likely to be destined, I turned my horse homeward, after first making for the beach where the riding would be easier than on the wandering sand hills of the interior. Ariel was one of the shaggy wild horses whose ancestors had been marooned on Sable more than a century ago. Though we kept busy with the many chores of the lifesaving stations, there was a good deal of empty time in which to ride, to read, to wander the island, or to sail the little lake in a skiff that we had salvaged from a wreck. One of the many phantasies that grew out of my reading was the notion that Father was a magician, exiled on a lonely island with his daughter, and surrounded by spirits that did his bidding. Such were my thoughts as we trotted home through the surf. It made me smile a little at the silly conceits of my youth, and yet I could not help imagining that this ship, which kept drawing closer, might carry a Ferdinand who would break the spell of our routines, and somehow transport me away from the life I knew.

The rescue stations had recently been connected with telephone lines, and soon – from the east light to the west – they had heard the news, those nearest turning out in time to see three boats coming in from where the steamer was moored offshore. Five of the rescue crew had come to watch, and eventually Father emerged from his study to provide a disapproving audience for our speculations as to what errand had brought our visitors. The consensus was that they most likely came to round up some of the wild horses to sell, as occasionally happened; but Father tended to view the unforeseen with an eye for portents, and refused to guess the meaning.

Despite the sun, it was a cold April day, and the north wind was blowing up whitecaps on the waves. The oarsmen looked less than pleased that they had to leap into the icy sea to drag their boats ashore, but the breakers were high and there was no other way.

In addition to the sailors who were manhandling the boats, a young gentleman was among the visitors, he obviously being the purpose of the voyage. It seemed that he was loathe to soak his feet, for he leapt from the bow of his boat onto the sand.

Discerning Father to be the one in charge, the young man addressed him cordially.

"Do I have the pleasure of meeting Dr Eusebius Ketchum?" he asked, extending his hand.

Father accepted it, but only nodded. They presented a strange pair: the young man of slight build, dressed in a fine suit, mild featured and winsome, while Father towered impassively over him by a good six inches, with the blowing black beard of an ancient patriarch, and the sturdy frame to match. They seemed to stare at each other for an unnaturally long time, the young man smiling and Father frowning, but neither man turned away.

"Doesn't do to get the feet wet when travelling; draws vital heat away from the body."

The remark annoyed Father for some reason, and he deepened his scowl. The young gentleman examined his shoes briefly to confirm their dryness, and brushed fitfully at his coat, presumably to improve its travelworn appearance.

"My name is Maddox. I've come to perform some research. This letter from the Lieutenant-Governor gives permission for my presence on the island, and requests any assistance that you may be at liberty to offer, sir, understanding of course that your lifesaving duties have priority."

Father took the letter, but merely grunted by way of response. I suggested that Mr Maddox and the other men should come indoors to warm themselves once their cargo was extracted from the boats. We rarely used much formality, and it seemed to me that the young man thanked me with peculiar warmth. I was pleased that these strangers were friendly and polite people. At least, the young man certainly was. Father often painted rather unflattering pictures of the outside world and of its evils, but Mr Maddox struck me as very agreeable. On an impulse, I decided to remain and watch the unloading. Father had returned to his studies, already bored with the distraction.

"Will you be staying with us for long?" I inquired of Mr Maddox.

"Just for a few days, while the conditions are right. I've arranged for another passing ship to pause here long enough to return me to England. My name is Rafe, by the way."

"Violet," I replied, taking the hand he offered.

"It must be a very lonely life for you here, Violet."

"At least, there are few opportunities for sin."

"Few opportunities of any sort, I would think."

"I do study a great deal. Our work in the lifesaving stations is also very important, you know. But there are times… do you have many friends Mr, or rather, Rafe?"

"Why, yes, I suppose I do. And colleagues. I'm fully occupied sometimes, just trying to answer the letters they send me."

For some time he had been watching me with a curious expression, and he suddenly laughed.

"You know, I hadn't expected to meet a young woman at this lonesome place, and one so…"

For some reason he did not finish his thought, smiling foolishly instead. Since I had been wondering on the subject, I asked what the conditions were that his research required.

"Well, the sun has periods of exceptional activity, and one such phenomenon has recently occurred. It takes a few days for the effects to reach us, because of the distance. Still, when it arrives, there is expected to be a large quantity of electrical disturbance in this vicinity. The remoteness also has its advantages. Generally, this seemed an ideal location, and time."

"The activity is related to sunspots, is it not?"

Mr Maddox replied with a gratifying expression of surprise, or perhaps of pleasure, and explained some of the mechanics of his experiment, which were intriguing.

"If I can be of any assistance, please let me know. I helped to install the telephone system between the lifesaving stations, and have some small knowledge of electrics."

By the time all of the equipment was dragged above the high tide mark, the sun was sinking. We continued our discussion of scientific matters as I led Mr Maddox to the house, where we could escape the increasingly cold winds. While the view from the parlour window faded in the dusk, we lit lamps to drive away the gloomy grey twilight. As our house was not a large one, from where I prepared dinner in the kitchen I could hear Father and Mr Maddox conversing, or failing to, in the next room, the talk consisting mostly of remarks on meteorology. It was as I was laying the table for dinner that Mr Maddox suddenly went out, returning a few moments later dragging a crate from the pile of goods that he had brought ashore.

"Almost forgot this, but the clatter of the china brought it to mind. A little gift for you, Dr Ketchum, by way of making up for some of the inconvenience of hosting me here."

There was a squeak of pried wood, and the clink of glass.

"Hmm. French Wine. Bordeaux. Haven't had any in years, not since before Violet was born."

"Yes, it's from 1851, before the *phylloxera*."

"Eh?"

"A pest, which ruined many vineyards, back in the '60s."

"Ah, didn't know about that. Thank you."

I dusted off a third place setting and, when everything was prepared, suggested that we should have some of the wine with our meal, as I had never tasted any such drink before, though it was often mentioned in literature. Once Father had said grace his preferred way, in Coptic, Mr Maddox wrestled with one of the bottles and, with a good deal of grimacing, tore the cork from it using some type of curious implement. The gentlemen drank their portions with every sign of satisfaction. Though I found the flavour strangely like a medicinal tincture, I did not wish to give offence to Mr Maddox, so I complemented his gift just the same. Surprisingly, once we had tucked into our ham and potatoes, and sampled a few more glasses, it seemed that the Bordeaux's taste grew more pleasant, no doubt due to those properties of wine which are said to improve upon exposure to air. Father's mood also improved. At any rate, it was certainly the case that he became more talkative than was usual for him.

"Not the sort of posh repast you're used to, I suppose," Father remarked, I think a little unkindly, to Mr Maddox.

As the gentleman had been looking slightly distressed, I supposed that my cooking was rather too simple for a man of his sophistication.

"Excuse me? No, no, it's excellent. Miss Violet has done a wonderful job. I was merely wondering, does the house always *move* like this?"

Father smiled, an expression that did not come frequently to him.

"Of course it does. It's just the wind. Creaks and groans a bit, but naught to worry about. Except in a gale perhaps. Could get blown out to sea then."

Father may have been exaggerating the danger a trifle. There were never any houses blown right off of the island in my recollection.

Returning to his favourite subject, Father sought to draw news of the world out of Mr Maddox, seeking hints of the events predicted in the scriptures that he studied. We learnt of the troubles in France following the recent war, and of other happenings that appeared to interest him.

"Have you read the Apocalypse of St. Thomas? You must; there is so much that makes no sense until you do."

"I've never come across it, to be honest. Not really my field."

"No, no of course not. I suppose I have the only copy, in any case."

They returned to the parlour to chat further, while I cleared the table and washed up in the kitchen. When I rejoined them by the parlour fire, we listened to Father describing his recent translations as we enjoyed another glass of the fine Bordeaux. Scholarly companions were rare indeed on Sable, and it had been my hope that Father and Mr Maddox would become friends, but unfortunately the young man appeared exhausted by his journey, for his eyelids were drooping. By way of reviving him, I raised the subject of his researches.

"What do you hope to find if your experiments are successful, Mr Maddox?"

He seemed momentarily confused, but soon recovered.

"My experiment? It pertains to the ether, its properties, and ... morphology. Re-coalescing latent forms in the ether."

I admit that I could make little of his explanation, but at least he was alert again. However, Father soon channelled the conversation back towards *his* interests. It was marvellously warm, and Mr Maddox seemed to much enjoy Father's discourses, often turning to me to inquire as to my thoughts. But it was Father's special area of study, of course, and I had little to add. Soon it was well past our usual bedtime. The three of us sat, a little mesmerised by the fire and the magic lantern show it cast across the walls, when Father suddenly put down his glass and split the silence with a singular question.

"Do you believe, young man?"

Even I, who was used to Father's intense nature, was taken

aback by the weight of his gaze on Mr Maddox. Father's face was quite flushed and excited.

"What do you mean, sir?"

"Eschatology, man, the Judgement Day. It's coming, you know."

"I confess, sir, that I am a man of science, and my knowledge does not run deep in religion. However, my work does touch upon the spirit world. My colleagues and I pursue such knowledge, calling our association the Etheric Explorers Club."

"A club, you say? What do they say at your club about the return of Yaldabaoth?"

"Yaldabaoth? Isn't that a myth of some sort? A bronze-age god?"

"Myth? Nonsense! All your science is insubstantial next to such a myth!"

Father snorted, but Mr Maddox was conciliatory, and he appeared to have wakened fully now. As if to snuff out any distractions, a chance draught flared the lamp up momentarily, and then extinguished it.

"Do tell me more, then. I confess I am quite ignorant of the subject."

The terrible intensity that I had seen earlier in Father's eyes returned, greater even than before, and I think that both Mr Maddox and I felt a slight chill in our hearts under the gaze. For my part, I drew a shawl tightly about my shoulders for reassurance, and listened as he spoke on about this strange ancient entity.

"Over twenty-five years I have spent, teasing out the story of Yaldabaoth from the scattering of fragments left. What the world knows of religion is merely a half-truth, just an inkling of the reality. Before our world was created there was only Sophia, infinite in wisdom and potential. She gave birth to Yaldabaoth. He is known by many other names. Allah. Jehovah. God. The jealous and vengeful God of the Israelites, who created the world, and destroyed it in the Flood. His breath brought the clay to life as Adam and Eve. He divided man from woman. But so mercurial, so fierce was his rule, that Sophia bound him in the lowest of the seven lower heavens. Before his banishment, he was permitted to leave a son behind on Earth, Yeheshua. Yeheshua lived as a man for a short time before he was put to death, and returned to the highest of the seven upper heavens, but in that time he repudiated the vengeful rule of his Father. His time as a man taught him compassion, and forgiveness. At the End of Time, Yaldabaoth shall be released, and Yeheshua will return to the Earth. The two will struggle for final control of the world in a great battle, beginning in the Holy Land, ultimately despoiling much of the world. Each will enlist his followers to take up arms on his behalf. The dead, too, shall rise from their graves and take sides, joining the living on the fields of battle."

Such was the conviction in Father's voice, I could not help but shudder at the vision he called up in our minds of that dreadful day. Mr Maddox, too, was not unaffected, seeming to grow pale in the firelight. Huddled in that small glowing circle, surrounded by the merciless sea, with the wind battering the thin walls, one keenly felt the frailty of man compared with the great forces at work in the world. Mr Maddox shifted restlessly, and Father continued, evidently quoting from one of the scrolls he had translated.

"The first chain of the confinement of Yaldabaoth, the veil of the lowest of the seven lower heavens, known as Tartaros, shall yield on the longest day, and Ireneaus, the bride of Yaldabaoth, shall rejoice, leaping at dawn above the world in her white cloak of stars. The seven heavenly portals shall yield unto his six-winged seraphim, the two guardians of each veil, female and male, opening each two years one gate of heaven, until the seven lie unbarred to Yaldabaoth, who shall walk upon the earth. Then shall the unrighteous give tongue to great lamentation."

"And you believe that this will happen sometime in the near future," asked Mr Maddox, in a voice hollow with tension.

"Back in Egypt, in the '50s, I could see it was coming. I just couldn't put a date on it. Not until after we had come here. In '61 the sign came. Comet Tebbutt, they called it. It was the sign of Yaldabaoth passing the first veil. She first appeared at dawn, stretching right across the morning sky from one horizon to the other, on the solstice. There's no doubt about it."

Though I was slightly muddled by the late hour, a quick calculation ran though my mind.

"But Father, that means the seventh veil would be lifted twelve years later. This year."

He nodded, looking down into his wine.

"This desolate place did not become our home by a mere whim, Violet. For many years I have seen the end coming. I had hoped that your mother and I would... that the horror of the Final Battle would pass by this place as it raged across the world. And when you were born, I wanted only for you to be spared. It would be an awful thing to witness such a contest, the living and the dead, grappling with each other and with the angels, giving no quarter until all is laid waste."

Father seemed mesmerised by the macabre tableau in his mind's eye. Neither I nor Mr Maddox could give voice to our thoughts, trying as we were to resolve whether this fate could truly be in store for us. This was the first time I had ever heard Father make so dire and definite a forecast, his usual manner being to split the details of his work finer and finer until I could not grasp the meaning of any of it. He departed abruptly, seemingly overcome by the inexorable future he foresaw, leaving us to brood on his vision until we retired.

On our journey the next day to the tip of the island, we did not immediately return to the previous night's discussion, which seemed all the more remote now beneath the uncharacteristically blue sky. And yet, by his distant manner I discerned that Mr Maddox, or Rafe, as I had begun to address him, had no doubt passed an unquiet night in the guest house next door, staring into a darkness filled with the senseless noises of the wind. As had I, for Father's sudden revelation had oppressed me all through the fretful hours before dawn.

It struck me that the six or seven miles were a needless distance to travel, but I supposed that there was some purpose to it, if only to be farther from Father, who had been very ill-humoured that morning, refusing even to wish the enterprise well. Nevertheless, he consented to my joining the expedition, if only to avoid any delay in its departure.

Accompanying us were two of the rescue crewman, driving the waggon that carried the many crates of apparatus for Rafe's research. The journey was raising their spirits, for the men, normally dour and quiet, seemed quite transformed, elbowing each other and grinning over their little jokes nearly the whole way. Rafe, though, largely defied my attempts to draw him out of his funk.

"Not foot-sore yet?" I asked, for Rafe had refused the pony offered for his use. Walking, I learned, was one of his many enthusiasms, or as Father would put it, peculiarities. The magnetic hat that he wore was another, and one which I still do not fully understand.

"No, no not at all," he replied vaguely.

Looking ahead, the gentle convexity of the strand hid our destination in the west, but from his gaze I could see that Rafe was brooding on something else: the skeletal wreck sprouting through the foam just offshore.

"That's *Stranger*. A brigantine. She was wrecked in the Summer of '66. I was only eleven then, and wasn't allowed to help when there was a ship in distress, but I remember the commotion when she ran aground. *Ephesus*, a steamer, foundered that same year, a little farther west. We might see some of the ribbing after another mile or so."

"Does it not seem a cruel fate, Violet, for the victims of these wrecks to lie as bones in the ocean until the end of time? Would that be the work of a benevolent God, or of a monster, the Yaldabaoth your father spoke of?"

"I should think we shall all end as bones somewhere or other, and yet most do not find it to be especially cruel."

"But to be cut off in mid-voyage, in the midst of who knows what sorts of hopes or anticipations, and plunged alone into the cold depths; is that not a terrible end?"

"Perhaps it is our pride that makes these accidents seem unnatural. Nothing is ever so under our control as we imagine."

"What fragile and fleeting creatures we are, that can be undone by a strip of sand in the sea."

While many of our more sensitive visitors were affected by the romantic melancholy of the island, Rafe's manner suggested such sincerity of feeling that it sparked a certain sympathy in me, for I felt that it was perhaps the surfacing of some long submerged longing at which I could only guess.

"We must have faith that a caring eye watches over us, even in catastrophe."

He half-turned a hard expression towards me before his features dropped and he looked out upon the wreck once more. For a moment I imagined that the young gentleman was weeping, until I realised that the grains in the wind must be troubling his eyes.

"The sands here can be very troublesome when a gust whips them into the air. I hope your eyes are not too bothered by it."

He rubbed at them for a moment, and laughed.

"Yes, I've begun to feel as though I've been scoured from head to foot. How do you stand it? Surely it isn't like this every day?"

"I'm afraid it is. However, I find that one may avoid a great deal of discomfort by simply wearing elastic undergarments. They're marvellous for keeping out the sand."

Not unexpectedly, the long walk had tired Mr Maddox's legs, for he stumbled and fell, almost certainly getting yet more sand into his clothes. The waggon-driver and his companion, though, were very unkind to snicker at Mr Maddox as they did. After all, they had been riding comfortably the whole way.

At the end of the island there was a small and weathered house, scarcely more than a shed, which was built to afford shelter to any who might find themselves abandoned by fortune there. One side was largely buried in drifted sand, but luckily the door was not blocked. Inside, there was enough room for Rafe to take some rest, but space for little else, for what volume there was had been taken up by stores laid in for marooned seafarers, along with a small stove and wood for heat. The visitor was rewarded with a singular view from that spot, overlooking as it did the very tip of the island, where a spine of shipwreck debris had formed along the axis of the land, and the bar could be seen extending for miles out to sea in a long line of churning white breakers.

"Why do you dangle everything from the ceiling?" he asked, rubbing his brow where it had collided with a ham.

"The rats. They'll eat anything not hung from a rope. Or locked in a steel chest. I don't suppose they'll bother you too much though."

As his crates were unloaded, joining a pile of lumber brought there earlier in preparation for the construction of the new west lighthouse, I asked Rafe how his experiment was to proceed.

"First I need to lay copper wires over several hundred yards, to gather charge from the rays emanating from the sun. That will power the equipment. Then, when the conditions are correct, I will tune the apparatus and observe the results."

"You might use rockets to lay the wires," I suggested. "We have a large supply. They're used for carrying rescue lines out to sea from the shore. I'm sure the same principle would work for wire. It might be faster than dragging the wire over the dunes."

At this suggestion, he gave me another of his quizzical looks.

"You know, you're the first young woman I've met who has a knowledge of rocketry."

"Is it a more typical pastime of old women in England?"

Rafe merely laughed, and continued unpacking his devices. We settled down upon the crates to take our luncheon once the cargo had all been examined for damage. The driver and his companion looked dubiously at the American silver dollars Rafe gave them before they started back to the main station. Foreign coins were no longer taken as legal tender, but he persuaded them it was the only money he carried. At any rate, a bank in Halifax would be bound to exchange the coins. It was, after all, a generous payment for a few hours' labour.

"Your work relates to electricity in some way, I take it," I inquired.

"In a manner of speaking, yes. Are you familiar with the calculus? You might find Maxwell's treatise on electromagnetism engaging. I have some galley proofs somewhere that he sent to me. Perhaps you would like to have a look at it while I am engaged with my apparatus? Yes, here it is, in my portmanteau."

Naturally I assented, though I had little doubt that the dog-eared bundle of sheets was beyond my understanding. Regardless though, I welcomed the opportunity to be amongst the first to read the treatise. Professor Maxwell is, after all, one of the greatest scientists of our age.

We ate for a while in silence, watching as a dark wall of fog approached from the sea. I could imagine how dishevelled Rafe was going to become, living out here even briefly. Already his black hair was tousled and full of grass and seaweed. Something – perhaps it was the grimaces he made when his teeth ground against the grit in his bread – suggested that he was not entirely suited to life in wild places. Men of science often make remarkable journeys to further their knowledge, but I could not help thinking he would much rather be back in London already, reporting his findings to some learned society, instead of perching on a dune in the Atlantic.

"I'm sorry if the food is a little abrasive. It isn't easy to keep the sand out. You must be used to living in much finer conditions than these."

"Don't apologise, Violet. Good company improves the worst trip. I'm afraid I'm just a little pre-occupied with my research. There is so much to do, and time is an unyielding master. I hope a storm will not interfere. Some of my devices are quite sensitive to rain."

No sooner had Rafe set down his bread and cheese, when Ariel, who had been edging closer to us for some time, stretched out his nose to eat up the leftovers. Far from being put out, Rafe found it rather amusing. Nevertheless, it was not a habit I liked to encourage in a horse, and so I shooed him away once he was done eating.

"If there is any help I can offer you, Rafe, I would be more than happy to aid you in your experiments. It's an opportunity I'm unlikely to have ever again."

"That's very kind, Violet, but there is a great deal of power involved, and it wouldn't be right to expose you to the danger. I even left my assistant behind in England, so you see that it's better for me to do this alone."

I should have liked to have participated, but still there could not be any harm in watching from a distance. This suggestion, however, did not meet with any more success than the last.

"I'm afraid I must insist that no-one be in the vicinity when the time comes," he told me, looking at his watch reflexively, as if some critical moment were fast approaching.

As you might imagine, this came as something of a disappointment to me. However, as my assistance was neither desired nor required, there was little purpose in my remaining.

"Since you are resolved to work alone, Mr Maddox, I should return to my chores at the rescue station."

"You're very welcome to stay and observe the preparations, Violet, if they interest you ..."

"No, no, I mustn't intrude on your time any further, sir. No doubt it's safer for me to be content with my homely duties. I'm sure there are rocket charges to test, or frozen mariners to drag from the tossing surf."

As he would be spending the night alone on that frightening promontory, I felt it only fair to set his mind at ease about the local legends before leaving.

"Before I go, I should assure you that there is no truth in the superstitions men hold here about the horrible visitations."

"Visitations?"

"Yes, have you not heard? Simple folk hold that there is a spectre, a murdered woman, who visits houses on lonely parts of the island. Apparently she shows people the bloody stumps of her fingers, which were cut off by wreckers as they stole her rings. It's all nonsense of course. Good luck with your experiments Mr Maddox."

There were not, in fact, many tasks demanding my attention when I returned, though Father was prowling restlessly about the house waiting for me to arrive. He instructed me rather severely to have nothing further to do with Mr Maddox. Though I did not say so, I suspected that he resented having spoken so passionately in front of a stranger, and blamed Mr Maddox for the whole affair. It only increased his peevish mood when I conceded that the matter was moot in any case, for I was already forbidden from approaching the site of the experiment.

An evening spent immersed in his books mellowed Father's wrath a little. Something in his manner, though, hinted at a scheme in his mind. Unusually, he was installed in the parlour, reading as if he intended on staying up to guard the front door the whole night, though whether it was to keep Mr Maddox from entering, or to stop my escape, was not clear. Until then I had merely been musing to myself about going out, but this unseemly suspicion convinced me of the virtue of a brief excursion. Still, there was the problem of how to get past Father. Reminding him of the late hour failed to send him off to bed. There was opium in the medicine chest of course, but it did not seem right to drug Father's tea, even if he was being bothersome. Then I remembered the ropes I had in my room for knot-practice, and an idea came to mind. In preparation, I brought a little candle-wax upstairs to lubricate my window.

After what seemed like hours of noisome waiting, the creaks and groans of floors and doors told me that Father had finally given up his watch and gone to bed. I lingered a little longer, for I knew that he was perfectly capable of knocking on the door with some ludicrous question or other, using it as a pretext for seeing if I were actually in bed. No knock came though, and I silently slipped out the window, with the gathering wind an excellent cover for any slight sounds.

My neck grew sore, but for the long dark ride I could hardly tear my eyes from the northern sky. Long shimmering tendrils of green and red jumped and played across the heavens, the brightest aurora that I had ever seen. Rafe was certainly correct concerning the activity of the sun, if that was indeed the cause of this colourful display.

Approaching the island's western terminus, the first impression I had of anything amiss was a queer sensation, almost of goose-flesh, as if there were electricity in the air. Since the night was moonless and I had been riding in the dark for some time, my eyes could also make out the faint warm glow just beyond the black silhouetted dune that edged the beach, dimmer than the aurora, but definitely coming from the land rather than the sky.

I tethered Ariel to a chunk of wreck near the shore, for I would not have him wandering too near to wires or other dangers. Scrambling up the face of the dune, I began to hear the faint thrum coming from the other side, rising and falling in the wind. From the top, lengths of dimly luminous wire could be seen extending from a control box like two great arms reaching out to embrace something coming from the sea in the west. It was an image I immediately tried to forget, for on such a night I did not like to think on what leviathans might dwell out there.

At the controls, buffeted by the gale, I could see Rafe moving his lantern for a better view of some bit of his machinery. Making nothing of it, I crept closer, sliding down one dune and climbing up the next, for it hardly seemed worth travelling so long only to learn nothing of what was happening. Suddenly Rafe appeared vexed, making numerous rapid adjustments at several boxes that were connected to the wires, and for a moment he held a great loop of wire up over his head while consulting something in his hand. Throwing it aside with evident frustration, he looked about him as if searching for something, and then returned his attention to the boxes. For some time I watched, all the while having the odd feeling of glimpsing something in the corner of my eye, only to find nothing there when I turned to look. Just when I had begun to believe that my imagination was betraying me, I could see what it was: the beach was moving. Or rather, something was moving over it. Faintly luminous, they were very nearly the size of apples. The things almost covered the beach, while a few drifted aimlessly across the dunes, one coming quite close to my foot. Only now could I recognise them as moon snails, a common sight along these waters, but these specimens were ephemeral, as if made from mist and pale light.

Perhaps Mr Maddox was really more of a Prospero than my father was, despite appearances. Certainly what I was witnessing was closer to magic than to any scientific experiment I had ever read of. Cautiously, I poked at the giant snail, but felt only air and sand, along with a barely perceptible ticklish sensation. Despite the peculiarity of it all, I couldn't help but laugh as a phantom sea gull appeared, swooping in a graceful loop over my head, only to disappear just as abruptly behind the neighbouring dune. Seeing a translucent seal scampering out of one dune and through another, as if it were as insubstantial as a cloud, I stifled another laugh, not wishing to reveal myself by a careless noise. Obviously Rafe preferred to keep this singular display of his a secret for some reason, but I was too curious as to how he could possibly be creating such elaborate illusions to simply watch from a distance. How foolish it seemed, for him to travel so far for the sake of staging such a frivolous and inexplicable spectacle without even an audience!

Gradually I crept nearer the centre of the activity, being careful to remain hidden amongst the curves and hollows of the sand. As I did, mobs of snails floated sluggishly past in every direction, while walrus sometimes materialised here and there, and a growing circle of gulls and terns flocked overhead, wheeling around and around over Rafe's device. Just as I began to grow accustomed to the odd menagerie, I gasped as two dolphins burst out of the sand at my feet, diving immediately down again. But I am not ashamed to relate that a yelp of alarm passed my lips as the dolphins were followed by the rising bulk of a great whale, its immense mouth agape as if to swallow me. Fortunately, the ghostly creature passed harmlessly over my body and vanished into the earth, and my cry was lost on the wind.

As I lay hidden in a patch of vetch, overlooking the last dune, I gazed towards the clearing that bore Rafe's control boxes and was impressed again with what an amazing fellow he was. He might instead be in London or New York, astonishing lords and million-aires with his efforts. But then, as a wealthy man, he had no need to peddle his arts except to receive popular admiration, something he seemed to value no more than the money he might earn. In the midst of such thoughts, I spied yet another species of illusion scrabbling forward. From its uncouth posture I took the thing to be some type of ape, for it was bent low over a pair of thin and bandy legs, but as I regarded it I realised what I took to be its pelt was in fact great masses of unkempt hair, and ragged clothing. A man! The wretch looked wildly around himself as he staggered past, turning a hollow toothless face to me before shuffling away in the direction of the beach.

Just as the artist often has a shadowy side to his nature, and every carnival has its house of horrors, so I suppose it should not have come as a surprise that Rafe's machine could conjure up fear-ful sights as well as delightful ones. Hardly knowing what to ex-pect, I awaited the next manifestation, but instead of continuing to operate the controls of his apparatus Rafe manoeuvred around them towards the sloping beaches at the westernmost point of the island and simply stood there, looking out to sea. What he saw, I could not tell, for it was only a black void of crashing waves to me. A luminous crab distracted me momentarily, scuttling through my arm, and when I turned back to Rafe I noticed that the waves were dashing over another phantom man who had appeared beyond him, out in the water. The fellow was no more troubled by the high seas than you or I would be by a heavy mist. He trudged up on to the land, more like him now surfacing and wandering ashore. Rafe walked down to the beach and approached each of them as they arrived in a manner that suggested he was welcoming them to the island, such that for a moment I though he must be mad. Or was it that he wished to inspect his handiwork?

The truth then struck me like an unseen rock, and yet I could hardly believe it. With a *frisson* of shock, the certainty crept over me that these glowing forms were not tricks at all, but spirits of the dead. All of them – the snails, the birds, these men – they were all creatures who had perished on these shores, now somehow summoned by Rafe's machine back into, if not life, then at least into some type of existence. Quickly, I glanced around me to be assured that none were approaching, for the thought of them drifting through me was now accompanied by a sort of horror. The dishevelled man earlier must have been some shipwrecked sailor from long before the rescue stations, or perhaps one of the convicts stranded here long ago by the French. Who could imagine what thoughts or impulses drove their wanderings after they materialised? Were they as senseless as beasts, or was there some understanding in them? Now at least it was clear what Rafe's motive was in performing his experiment. From the way he was darting amongst the spectres on the beach, there was someone in particular that he was seeking, someone who must be the purpose of this expedition. A loved one perhaps? The morbid focus of his earlier thoughts on the wrecks offshore now began to make more sense. The loss, and this anticipated reunion, must have been long weighing on his mind.

Realising that Rafe was actually summoning ghosts through natural philosophy cast such a newly urgent light on events that skulking in the grass no longer seemed quite an adequate response. Rafe carried on interviewing phantasms, oblivious to my approach until I was practically at his side, when he jumped with a startled shout.

"I should say by your excitement that you've seen a ghost, Mr Maddox, but then I would have to assume that you had grown used to that by now."

"Violet," he exclaimed, "you shouldn't have come here, the, the …"

"The electricity? The …," I wagged my hand in the direction of the heavens, "… solar forces?" I was about to remonstrate him for the scientific smokescreen he had employed to distract us from his real purpose, when I saw that I was waving my hands at a quite indescribable scene in the black sky. From Rafe's dumbfounded expression I divined that it was none of his doing, or at any rate nothing that he had anticipated.

How shall I describe it? Drawn there in the air were two figures sketched on a vast scale, ephemeral, like the things moving about us, but infinitely larger and more detailed. Spanning a great height from the horizon to the clouds, they stood facing each other, a man and a women one might say from their unclad forms, though with strange bestial heads like lions, and many long wings like a swan's. These they crossed between them in a curious gesture, as if shaking hands. As we watched, the pair swelled, growing in both size and brightness, until they fairly filled the western sky.

"What the devil have you done?" I demanded.

"I'm sorry, I should have been honest with you. Generally no-one believes me when I discuss the true nature of my work. But this," he gestured at the apparition filling the sky, "was unexpected."

"Who did you come here to find?"

"Ellen. My sister. She was lost at sea here."

I nodded, understanding in a way. As we stood there, staring up at the awesome couple in the air, my thoughts turned again to my mother, wondering if Rafe's device might have the power of allowing me to meet her, as he hoped for it to bring back his sister. The figures meanwhile were performing what looked to be a slow and complex dance, until finally they turned to face us, with their wings touching between them in an arch.

"I think perhaps you should shut down your machine," I suggested, growing uneasy under the eyes of the huge figures. Rafe hesitated, looking again out to sea where phantoms continued to rise from the surf and float landward.

"Just a few minutes longer, Violet. I may never have this opportunity again."

Rafe moved a little farther out, into the mounting waves that were rolling up the beach and over our feet now. Beyond, a great swath of sea had become faintly phosphorescent, making it more difficult to pick out the features of the emerging ghosts. I was about to insist that Rafe cease his experiment at once, but a glimmer of light in the east caught my eye, and I squinted through the wind to see if I could discern what it was. Was it possible that the device's action worked in both directions, reviving souls there as well as here? The towering figures seemed distant and irrelevant now, eclipsed by my desire to find Mother, if Rafe's device had indeed set her to wandering the island. Yet a frustrating thought hovered just out of reach, some memory that felt important. Something from another night, not long ago. Was it last night? What had happened? We had enjoyed our dinner, and then gone to bed. Was that all? Perhaps the wine had made me forgetful. Though I scanned the bedlam of creatures floating all around, no face had appeared to match the photograph on the mantle at home.

All at once the seething hosts of phantom men and animals froze in their various meanderings, while the ring of wheeling birds dropped earthward. Like scattered iron dust twisting around a magnet, each one halted to turn its eyes towards the couple in the sky, whose arched wings now framed a space filling with light. My mind too was filling, with a babble of voices that bawled words I could not quite understand, but that seemed to be poisoned with contempt or anger, as if a thousand foreign children were berating their younger sisters. Rafe shook his head, his mouth moving soundlessly. To my alarm, I found that nothing but hollow breath came when I tried again to shout to him to shut down the machine. I am sure my own eyes gave silent voice to as much panic as did his, for when they met we both turned to rush for the control boxes, only to find ourselves paralysed somehow. As the raving voices began to drown out all other thought, I found my body moving stiffly of its own accord, with Rafe's mirroring every gesture. First we dropped onto bent knees. Our heads rose to peer up at the fantastical figures above.

For some while, exactly how long I cannot tell, we stared upwards together in a sort of dumb, terrified awe, of the type I imagine a devoted dog must feel for a brutish master. For a moment there was an aching pain when a flash of light came, and my view of the figures was blocked. Loud words were spoken nearby, strange and yet familiar words. Then, as quickly as waking from a dream, I found myself confronting Father, who was carrying a lamp and reciting monotonously, his voice now the only noise beside the wind. He turned to me, the prayer or incantation apparently finished.

"Didn't think you fooled me with that rope business, did you?" he asked.

A little disoriented, it took a moment for me to recall my escape.

"Your mother took the same route out of *her* father's palace in Cairo, when we eloped."

"Is this …" I began, pointing at the sky as I recalled Father's eerie tale the previous evening.

"Yes." He turned to Rafe. "If you've a hand in this, then for God's sake, or for ours, do what you can to stop it."

Once more free to think and move by his own will, Rafe sprinted up the dune for the controls while I followed close behind. Whatever was unfolding around us, and I now knew it to involve the apocalyptic scenario that Father had described, we sensed it was approaching a crisis. The need to act without further hesitation drove me to the small rescue house, where an axe lay amongst the provisions. Outside, the light had grown bright as twilight, fading the phantoms and casting long shadows over the sand. Father nodded approvingly at the sight of the axe in my hand. Mr Maddox, though, yelped and caught my arm as I started to swing the axe onto the controls with all of my strength. For an instant, I imagined he was again under the influence of Yaldabaoth, or whatever had been affecting us, but he explained his reluctance to smash the device.

"I've tried cutting the current – it has no effect. The manifestation must now have the power to sustain itself."

He was deflated by hopelessness, which Father did nothing to help.

"What a bloody fool you are, Maddox! I knew it the second I laid eyes on you," said Father.

But Maddox had a notion that set him to throwing switches and tuning the coils of the controls. "There's another possibility," he told us, explaining in a rapid pizzicato of jargon that I cannot even attempt to reproduce. The gist of it, though, was that just as he had built up a resonance in the ether, he could also set the machine to create an opposite field, or anti-harmonic effect, and thus dissipate the apparitions. This he attempted as we watched, unable to understand enough to lend him any aid. Father turned grimly to the sky again, where the gap between the seraphim had become a shimmering sheet of flame. The great figures stood oblivious to

Rafe's tinkering. When nothing came of his efforts, I began hefting the axe impatiently, as holding it was beginning to tire my arms. At first, I could see no changes, but then the crowds of phantoms flickered and dimmed. Rafe's theory was working after all!

It did not take long however to see that, though faded, the ghosts remained tenaciously even with the machine using all of its power to dissipate them. What is more, the seraphim had turned their eyes upon us, aware perhaps for the first time of our struggle to confound them.

"It's no good. I can't get any more power from it," Rafe told us.

Our wits dulled by exhaustion, we each tried to conceive of some alternate plan. Father suggested, somewhat unhelpfully, that we should prepare our souls for the next world.

Amid our deliberations, yet another spectre wafted from out of the dunes, looked about herself, and moved to intercept our little conclave. With a twinge of embarrassment and irritation I recognised, from the mutilated hands she was holding before her, that this was the spirit I had mentioned previously to Rafe: the unfortunate woman who had lost both her rings and her fingers to avaricious wreckers. She floated towards us in that terrifyingly in-exorable manner that tipsy bridesmaids have of approaching their victims, when they intend to inflict a maudlin cataract of tears upon someone. By now, however, none of us were in any mood for her morbid high jinks. Rafe and I merely exchanged glances before returning to the problem at hand, leaving Father to shoo her away impatiently. Eventually the ghost pursed her lips and de-parted, looking somewhat put out.

"What if the inductance … no. Or the sponge coil? No," Rafe mumbled, his mind flitting amongst the various intricacies of his device.

"Is there no way to increase the power?" I asked.

"No, it's drawing as much as there is."

"Could we not lay more wire, to gather power?"

"It took me hours of struggling over the dunes to lay what there is; there surely isn't time for that."

"You didn't use the rockets, as I suggested?"

Rafe looked slightly embarrassed.

"Well, that is, I … I am not entirely comfortable with …"

"You're afraid of rockets?"

"Not *afraid* exactly; there was this incident, you see, with some explosives. They're not exactly my forté."

"But in principle ..."

"Yes, yes, it might ..."

"Oh, for heaven's sake," shouted Father. "Just do it, if you're going to do *anything!*"

His tone of impatience was not merely his usual self. Father had seen what Rafe and I now beheld with dismay, not immediately understanding what it signified. Running to the rescue house for rockets and spare wire, we noticed the odd motions in the sands wherever our eyes fell. Grains shivered into the air, some borne away on the wind, some coalescing into amorphous shapes, coming apart, and joining together again. Not until whole bones appeared, did we fathom this latest phenomenon. Evidently the seraphim were surpassing Rafe, resurrecting the dead in a more substantial form so as to frustrate our efforts, or worse.

Each rocket was mounted on a stick, which we hastily drove into the sand near the control boxes. In place of the usual rescue line, we attached the end of a wire, uncoiling the rest into a loose pile on the ground that could be carried away quickly by the rocket. It was difficult to concentrate on the task, for the blowing sand was an annoyance. Moreover, the things taking shape out of bone and dust could hardly be ignored. Perhaps seeing our distraction, Father retrieved the axe from where I had dropped it.

"You two look to your work. I will attend to the rest."

He strode away, leaving us to finish the assembly. We had more rockets than we could conceivably use, but only enough wire for six, so at least if one misfired, we could try again. If there were time. Three rockets pointed north-west, and three south-west, their wires all linked to the ether machine. Only when they were all prepared did we think of the need for matches. Rafe luckily had a box in his coat pocket, which he passed to me.

Above us, lightning was jumping amongst the storm clouds that were smothering the last patches of aurora. It had seemed so spectacular not long ago. Great peals of thunder were punctuating the wail of noise from the portal, howling now like a choir of discord. In the portal's flames, something was emerging that was terrible to witness. When I tried to look, it felt as though my eyes were crossed and aching. One felt drawn to it, nevertheless.

It was all we could do to keep the matches alight long enough to touch the fuses, but after a dozen were spent the first two rockets were aloft bearing their wires out to the edge of the island. The next pair were as hard to light as the first, and in the midst of it a fleshless hand seized Rafe about the neck, dragging him away from me. It was a grey and headless skeleton of a man, but Rafe seemed to be a match for it, for he shouted that I should finish with firing the rockets, before he disappeared behind the dune in a flailing tangle of limbs and bones. It seemed the best course, for the clouds were spattering down rain that grew heavier each moment. Soon nothing would burn. Already one rocket was too damp, and had to be replaced.

As if in triumph, the cacophony from the seraphim was swelling to a maddening shrillness. I had practically to wrap my body about the rockets to shield them enough to light, and leapt away when the fizzling orange trail shot up the fuses. Two more were launched. Laughing a little hysterically, I shook the matchbox at the portal until I realised I was foolishly getting it soaked in the rain. Sobering up, I set to lighting the last two rockets, which finally flew away as the last of the matches were spent. Rafe re-appeared now, having got the better of his opponent as I had known he would. He went at once to the controls, choking a little from his throttling.

"This rain won't help matters," he told me. "The instruments weren't meant to take this much power either."

He indicated the smoke and steam coming from the mahogany cases holding his apparatus. We desperately draped our coats over them, while rain streamed into our eyes. Through my blinking, I only once caught a glimpse of Father, who was on the beach below us, hacking at a group of boney men who rode skeletal ponies in circles around him. Lightning was striking so close to us now that we were nearly bowled over by the blasts of thunder.

The controls crackled and flickered below our coats with little arcs of electricity. The din of the portal rose suddenly and then snuffed out, leaving our ears ringing. We rubbed the rain from our eyes to see the two seraphim parting their wings. Slowly, almost imperceptibly, they turned their backs to each other and to the portal that had been forming between them, and as they faded the clouds parted, leaving us damp and shaking, beneath the aurora once more.

Rafe's machine was such a smouldering ruin that he chose to leave it behind on the island, where it eventually sank into the sand. I had imagined that Father would be quite cross at Mr Maddox for inciting the apocalypse in our back yard, but quite the contrary. In fact, he seemed exuberant afterwards, and made every effort to overcome Rafe's despair at both failing to find reunion with his sister and at his brush with disaster. By dawn, both were fast friends, laughing over the affair with a good number of bottles of wine done in between them.

Rafe and I took to corresponding thereafter. With Rafe's help, I have been able to attend lectures at Newnham Hall, Cambridge, where I now reside. It is a stimulating environment, though slightly frustrating, for in a moment of madness I forced him to postpone his offer of marriage until the end of my studies. One hopes in future he will not be so rash in his experiments as in times past, but one cannot be too optimistic.

Cotton Avicenna B. iv.

or

The Alighieri Gloss

L ONDON! PARAGON OF cities. How many wonders there are, in its villas, its marketplaces, in its streets and tunnels. London — this uncommon weal of fateful miracles, and of horrors that I know only too well. Cheek by jowl a multitude lie, a thousand-thousand strange tales between them, unknown but for the chance mis-step into an unfamiliar alleyway — the passing glimpse along a half-lit, fog-swathed street. So has it always been in the great cities that draw in every kind of creature. Those who toil; those who live upon them. The builders, the wreckers. Town- and country-men. The eager, the wicked, the mad; and not from this isle alone, but from all the ends of the world. Indeed, not only from this… but now, let me see. How to begin.

Rafe — Dr Maddox — was leading me upon another tour of the city, the latest of our annual excursions that began after the blessèd meeting in Tower Tunnel. We viewed the palaces; of the Empress, of entertainment, of crystal, of iron and steam afloat on the Thames, and others among the marvellous constructions of the age.

Not the *Underground*, of course.

But no museum, no theatre brought us out that November night to St. Raphael Square. We went rather to the Etheric Explorers Club, for Rafe was to stage there a little show of his own. He called it *Cotton Avicenna B. iv. : A Novel Method of Revealing Decayed Calligraphy*. Something to do with books, he led me to understand.

Maddox is a great scholar, and much, much more.

Until the lamps were lowered, members and guests of that club had eyes only for myself, in my veil and mourning, try as they did to pretend otherwise. It was no surprise, as no other women were in attendance. None, at least, of which they were aware. For my part, I watched Rafe. It was strange that his was no longer a young man's face. He introduced me as his *niece!*

A magic lantern, he called it, this thing he used. Not *true* magic, he took pains to assure me, but rather a bright lamp and glasses that cast images over the wall. Images of writing. Magic, apparently, is no longer considered quite in good taste in this day and age; spirits are another matter.

"Here we see a photographic slide made using the red portion of the spectrum... and here the green..." he explained, switching between images which were, according to Rafe, slightly different.

A fat man across the table from me cleared his throat. "This mottling. It's due to the fire?"

Rafe paused. "No, not fire, Morrison. Damp. It's not widely known, but an ancestor of mine received the Avicenna manuscripts from Cotton's collection, in exchange for some debt or other — this was before the fire occurred. Also the eponymous bust. This particular volume," he said, touching a brown and scarred codex before him on the table, "is apparently an anthology of geographical works, collected in Arabic. I've yet to have it translated. It is the legibility of these glosses," he said, indicating the luminous scribbles with a stick, "in Medieval Tuscan, which I have been endeavouring to improve with my technique. It was only some years after the collection was split that the Ashburnham House fire occurred. I'm afraid that, since those days, my family has not always been conscientious in its care of the Avicenna manuscripts."

How typical it is of these obtuse, modern people, to deny the existence of fate and mystery to such an extent that they would consign a treasure trove of priceless books to a house with the inauspicious name *Ashburnham*. What did they expect would happen? Children, the lot of them. It's what comes of allowing immigrants to take over the country — these Jutes, and Angles, and sundry Saxons. The Norse men, and all the rest. No regard for the workings of fortune, any of them. No sense. At least Maddox is a scion of the true Britons, whatever else may be mixed into his blood.

We came, betimes, to the end of the talk. Rafe was attempting to disengage himself from an associate with a brass machine and the maniacal look of the enthusiastic inventor — a look with which I have become very familiar after several visits to this club — when the footman entered, bearing a card on a salver. He resembled a sad and dissipated legionary, this footman, and something about his silent, looming bulk made the inventor's gabbling tail away.

"Messenger for you, Dr Maddox."

Rafe took the card and examined it with slight interest.

"His master is waiting, Billingsly?"

"There is a carriage at the door, sir."

Rafe nodded. "Pack away my slides and projector, would you, Billingsly?" Taking Rafe's proffered arm, I accompanied him towards the doorman's nook, where a strange man in a colourful coat and short trousers stood. He did not look English, or even British.

The man bowed with sullen care. He wore an absurd white wig that was on the verge of tumbling off. A long queue of his own black hair ran down his back.

"Lord Mo Gui deeply regrets his being unable to attend tonight's lecture," said the man, thickly pronouncing the words with the same careful deliberateness with which he managed his wig. "Lord Mo Gui sends his carriage, and invites you to kindly do him the honour of accepting his hospitality this evening, to discuss certain facts concerning the ..." The man hesitated, dropping his eyes to the book tucked beneath Rafe's arm before enunciating "the *Cotton Avicenna B. iv*."

"How curious," said Rafe. "A student of ancient manuscripts, is he?"

"The master has special knowledge of it." He looked again to the book, though whether in questioning or covetousness I could not judge.

Rafe turned to me. "If you have no objection?"

I shook my veil.

Outside, the night street was alive with clattering wheels and iron-shod hooves. Foot-travellers surfaced in ones and twos at the gaslights, then sank back into the river of shadow.

"Whitechapel Slaying!" keened a child on the pavement, a bundle of papers piled in his arms. "Vigilence Committee Baffled!"

They can shout in square capitals, these modern Londoners.

As though overcome by his own eloquence, the boy's eyes fluttered, then rolled away, white, into his head. He tipped back in a rigid fit, nearly striking the pavement before Rafe caught him.

I watched, appalled. "Come away, Rafe! This is a black omen!"

My attention flew from the boy to the far street corner. A gaslamp had winked out. A couple, tall, fair, in dark cloaks rounded the turn.

"Rafe ..."

But he never heeds me. Instead, he carried the boy, with difficulty now the seizure was in full force, to the bland footman who still stood in the open club doorway.

The next streetlight died as the pair advanced. A hack-horse near the pavement lurched madly away from them into the traffic, hooves slipping, the cabman screaming.

"Rafe, we must go now."

"I can't stay, Billingsly," said Rafe, passing the shaking boy to him.

I sometimes wonder if that footman would so much as blink if one of the members plucked the Moon from the air and handed it to him for safekeeping.

"Get some brandy into him when he comes 'round. And give him this," said Rafe, depositing a couple of half crowns into the footman's pocket.

"Quickly," the gaudy messenger urged.

At the waiting carriage, Rafe assisted me inside while the messenger mounted hastily in front. Setting off into traffic, I touched the smooth window glass that showed the lighted street so agreeably even as it barred the smoke, and noise, and smell. The fair couple had stopped at the club doors, a row of dead lamps in their wake. They were watching us accelerate away. Rafe seemed not to have seen them in his preoccupation with the newsboy.

"That lad was ill-starred," I said. "You too often involve yourself in the affairs of others."

He turned to me from his own window. "*Homo sum: humani nil a me alienum puto*, as the Roman, Terence, said. I am a man — I think nothing of mankind is foreign to me. There is only one affair, Brenna, and we are all involved."

I suppose it is his religion that makes him do these inscrutable things. There being no purpose in probing strange beliefs, I went instead to practicalities.

"You're certain," I said, "that your *wife* does not object? To entertaining me?"

"Violet understands. She's a very modern woman."

I drew back my veil, to see the street-life the better. "Not like me, then."

Rafe's appraising eye fell upon me. "No," he said after a moment. "Not like you."

The book was on his lap now. He stroked the scarred leather. "Odd," he said, his voice lower now. "That Chinaman, in knee-breeches and livery. One doesn't see that much on anyone outside of court, much less on a Chinese fellow."

He lapsed into introspection. For my part, my mouth was soon stopped with awe of the city. So many passing faces, such shops and homes of brick and stone. Somewhere, the quarries and clay-pits must be dug down to the underworld to raise such a city. A vast, empty, anti-London. There is always a price. Always balance.

"I don't like the look of those columbia," I said, observing a ring of birds perched in a noose around a statue's neck.

Rafe sniffed.

"If we don't heed the signs, Rafe, we will fail to see what is in store for us. Like that one-eyed crossing-sweeper we saw crushed under the cab."

"What was *he* a sign of?"

"Of inattention."

Rafe drummed his fingers on the book.

"Brenna, I know I've sometimes asked before, but ..."

"You're wondering what it is like."

"There."

As with each time before, it was like grasping water.

"Like a dream. It slips away."

"Is there nothing? No way to compare it with ..."

"It is better."

After a time, Rafe grew restless in the silence, frowning and squinting out the windows. Finally he examined the card once more. "This isn't the way to Finsbury Square."

"Is it not? Look, there is The Tower." It had been my first sight of London. *This* London. An awesome sight.

"We're continuing eastward."

We passed streets that Rafe named, but which meant nothing to me. Houndsditch. Aldgate. Onto Whitechapel.

"Aldgate? Is that one of the wall gates?"

"It was."

"I remember the gates. Is there …?" I felt something. "A great pit of bones."

The suggestion slitted Rafe's eyes. Presently we left the street, turning into a tunnel-like carriageway, the close gloom sending shudders through me even as we emerged into a black-shadowed courtyard at the heart of an insula. Gates crashed together behind us in the alley, sealing the yard like a sepulchre…or columbarium.

Stopping, the carriage rocked as someone stepped from it onto crunching road-metal. The man in livery, a lantern in hand, released us.

"This way, sir, madam."

Rafe stepped down and assisted my exit. I took his arm once more and we fell into step with the lamp-bearer, passing into the house's dark corridors. Rafe's features pinched up in repugnance at the place. He hates the close dark. All smell is disease, they say, and all darkness evil. They are correct.

Finally, deep inside the edifice, the messenger knocked upon a scarred door, black with soot or paint. From within there issued a growling reply. "Come."

We were led into the fire-lit room, long and lively with shadows that hid much of the place, and sat in a pair of padded chairs near the middle of the chamber, facing a third at the far end where there was a great hearth. Logs of immense proportions blazed, crackling with a life so much more alluring than the stingy smoulder of coal grates. I ached to be near the flames, to be warm; even my veil, closed again, bent towards them, drawn by the fierce draught. But the way was blocked. A silhouette, rimmed in fire. A vast wing-chair, its back to the hearth; a large man was installed there, hidden in the lea of the chair.

"Welcome, Doctor Maddox," said the man, in a low voice, gravely, like a stone wall collapsing. "And guest."

Rafe leant forward, peering into the shade of the wing-chair. "Your Finsbury Square calling card address is a little out of date, Mr Hamilton. Or is it *Lord Mo Gui?*"

"That is what *they* call me," said the man, lifting a great hand from his chair in the direction of whatever dark corner his foot-man had retired to. "Something in their tongue. I find it convenient to keep servants who are … outsiders. They keep to themselves, and speak little English. I am Jock Hamilton, as my card states. Or *Jack*, as you English prefer." Rafe seemed about to comment when the man broke his pause. "I knew your grandsire, Maddox." A hacking rattle interrupted Hamilton. "And some of his little friends. The Athenians."

"Did you know that he still lives?"

"Does he, by gad? I expect he has changed a good deal in fifty-eight years. I know I have. Not so much *spring* in my heels as there was." Another rattle.

Hamilton clapped his huge hands, a sound like a falling body striking cobbles. In reply, a new servant appeared. "Pipe," ordered Hamilton. One was produced, and Hamilton drew through it the flame of a spill lit from the fire. He snuffed out the stick with his fingers and began a rhythmic tapping on the arm of his chair, the spill chattering like teeth against the furniture. But it was not the spill — he had dropped that. His nails made the noise. Of scuttling crabs.

A cataract of smoke spewed from the hidden old man, over the chair back and into the draught heading for the chimney, but a little of the reek of it reached us.

"It surprises me," said Rafe, "that you have lived this long, taking opium."

"*Madak*, rather, if you will allow me the nicety. But a man of your, ah, reputation, should not suffer to be surprised so easily."

As Rafe retreated back into his chair, considering this, he shifted his book from one hand to the other, bringing it momentarily into the firelight. Old Hamilton fell suddenly still, his nail-clatter silenced.

"Is that it? The *Cotton Avicenna B. iv.*?"

Rafe hesitated. "It is."

Hamilton twitched a finger. Behind us, bolts were slammed

home on the doors.

"Give it to me," growled Hamilton.

"What claim do you, sir, have ..." protested Rafe, stopping as another gesture from Hamilton brought his pair of servants slinking back into our circle of light. Rafe remained impassive, the liveried men advancing upon him, only at the last moment drawing long knives from beneath their embroidered coats.

Who can say whence comes strength on these occasions? The courage to carry on when violence bares its dreadful teeth? I cannot, though I have had occasion to regret past failures in the face of violence, failures that have long troubled me in the, the ... *leisure* that I have been afforded. Perhaps it was those regrets, and the desire to see them never repeated, which set me suddenly on my feet, my chair tumbling away behind me along with my veil. Those memories, propelling my left hand to the liveried messenger's wrist, crushing it like a reed, the dagger dropping to clatter on the floorboards. That resolve, driving my right fingers like porcelain blades through his neck before his shock from his broken bones had even turned to pain.

We were statues in the firelight, motionless but for the hot, sanguine cascade from the throat of the messenger, suspended limply now from my upraised arm, as if we two were the centrepiece of some terrible fountain.

In the stillness, the clacking of Old Hamilton's nails began again.

"Well," he said. "Well, well."

I was more concerned with the other servant, watching, his knife hovering uncertainly between Rafe and me. I let the messenger slip away into the dark pool at his feet.

Hamilton's clattering ceased. He shifted. I looked to the servant, waiting for his response to Hamilton's cue. Then, the old man leapt. Leapt! The ancient consumptive launched like a bolt from his chair, landing just short of me. He seemed exhausted by the effort, hunched, froglike on the floor, panting. Hamilton's face pressed the floorboards, prostrate in obeisance to ... what? His pale, coarse jaws worked, as if mumbling supplications.

He lapped ... blood. The messenger's warm blood.

The other servant stared from me to Hamilton, a great shudder racking his body as he understood what his master did. Eyes wild, he dropped his dagger and ran for the door, fumbling impotently with the bolts for so long I thought he must be mad. At last he worked the lock and was gone.

Hamilton took no notice.

I looked to Rafe. His face was set, thoughtful, watching the creature at our feet. Amid its slubbering, Rafe stretched out his legs, crossed his ankles, and inserted a pipe between his lips.

Even at a moment such as this ... This is an age of fire. The very people smoke.

Stuffed with tobacco, the pipe flared at the touch of a match, which Rafe tossed, sizzling into the puddle of gore.

"Hamilton!" barked Rafe.

The awful lapping slowed. Hamilton's head turned up, jowls crimson and oozing. Only now did we properly see his huge face. Swollen... hairless. Cadaverous.

"Pull yourself together, man," said Rafe. He waggled his pipe. "Have a smoke."

The... Hamilton looked about as if waking in strange chambers. His thick tongue darted out again to run along his lips. Straightening, he averted his eyes from Rafe, and from the messenger's jumbled body. He delved into a pocket, producing a handkerchief, wiping ineffectually at his face.

"Forgive me, I ... yes. A pipe," rumbled Hamilton. He threw away the soiled handkerchief and crossed to the doors, shutting and barring them once more, before leading us to carry our chairs over to the hearth. "Away from that," he said, a talonned hand twitching towards the body.

Once settled, Hamilton breathed a thin blue flame into the pipe to light the tobacco and opium, examining me the while.

"Now listen to me, Maddox. There may not be much time. You must give me that book at once."

Rafe's extraction of his pipe to protest was in vain.

"I know ..." Hamilton continued, "I am a thing to be despised. I despise myself. But the noose and the knife make no impression upon this hide of mine. Do not imagine that I've not tried, at times, in despair."

His gaze suggested that he wondered at the efficacy of my

hands.

"But why in heaven's name do you ..." Rafe began.

"The book. I know it. And curse it. For your own soul, and mine, and souls yet unborn, give it to me!"

"Why?"

Hamilton's features, already dreadful, assumed a vicious anger before he mastered his hate and groaned. Taking smoke from his pipe to steady himself, he growled on.

"We were mad for ancient things in those days. I understand your generation has surpassed the ancients in wonders. You look to the future. But then, it was ruins that caught the fancy of the young. Greece. Rome. The tombs of pharaohs. And old books... that book. Damn that book!"

"Not a classical work," Maddox interjected, "is it? Something Arabic."

"The glosses, fourteenth century. The text, oh, eighth century, perhaps. But the substance of it, Maddox. Far older.

"It was 1829 when I found it in your Grandfather's library. Borrowed it. Took it on my tour of Italy and the new Greek kingdom, or rather the relics they inherited. Had some notion of getting it translated in Stamboul. Until I met a Copt in Venice, a monk, who knew the language. He deciphered it." Hamilton seemed to stare away into infinity, or the distant past. "Then I tried to go through Delphi, but couldn't find the way. But there was another route. Near Parga. That was my first mistake." Again the old man rattled and coughed, unless it was laughter. Or a sob. "You've read the Italian, Maddox."

"The glosses, yes. Directions. Landmarks. Warnings. Is it an itinerary of some sort?"

"Of a sort. I compared them with a translated manuscript, now, alas, lost. They are directions, as you say. To, and through, a place with many entrances, few exits. There, I spent my life, and became ... this. Those glosses are in the hand of Dante Alighieri." Hamilton flung his pipe into the hearth. "For pity's sake, Maddox, give me the book!"

Rafe had already abandoned his own tobacco. "How many others have you sent there, *Jack?*"

A smirk disfigured the creature's face before Hamilton returned, in a melancholy I could well recognize. "I was not always thus, Maddox. It changes one. How could it not, fifty, sixty years in such a place. Even the body adapts, as much as flesh may," he said, examining his great clawed hands, "as Lamark thought."

"What is the main text, Hamilton?" demanded Rafe.

"The Orphic Mysteries, Maddox. The only surviving record. It is a guide to Hell."

We watched the fire, each guarding his own thoughts, until Rafe spoke again.

"But why do you need the book? Surely …"

Another groan, or sigh, wheezed out of Hamilton's bulk.

"I had no Virgil as guide, I was cheated, robbed, misled, and cruelly used from my first step. Only because I still live, after a fashion, may I come and go at all, for a few hours, or days, each year. There are tides in the affairs of men — isn't that said? So with the realms of the damned. Now weak, now strong, they ebb and swell with influence. Here, there, one foot in sun, one among the shades," Hamilton said, rattling again, "I feel every wax and wane." I stood as the old man reached out to seize Rafe's arm, but Rafe shook his head. "I swim against the current, Maddox," said Hamilton, "but it gets the better of me. For the love of God, believe me Maddox, I never meant to kill those women! But the appetites of that place … fifty years of hunger, man! There is no meat there but others' souls. I would never have kept returning here, but for the book! The book …" Hamilton fell to his knees before Rafe. "Give me the chance to find a way to Purgatory!"

Distantly, as though from the street or some remote corner of the house, a desperate cry sounded, just as abruptly cut off. Hamilton turned wildly to the doors.

"They've come, man. They've come for me. From *there*."

"Surely it was just … you mean they *follow you?*" Rafe stood, shaking off Hamilton's clutching nails at the expense of his sleeve to take a few hesitant steps towards the doors. One of the knobs turned, and rattled. I rose, Hamilton hopelessly following suit.

A great force struck the doors, splintering the wood in places. Rafe strode to them, with me on his heels, the next blow loosing a hinge. He was nearly upon them when the third attack burst the bolts, flinging wood and ironmongery past us, across the room, to where Hamilton cringed by the fire.

Filling the passage left by the doors were the fair couple in their black cloaks. They stirred, as if to enter, then kept their place. One inclined her head. She regarded me, then Maddox.

"Move aside. We want *him*." She pointed past us.

"I will not," said Rafe.

The other spoke. "This is not your affair … man."

Rafe took a step closer to the pair. "Do you know who I am?"

The two said nothing, but looked briefly to each other.

"I will not grant *you*," said Rafe, "what I denied to *Him*. You shall not enter this place."

The couple watched him in silence, making no move to advance or retreat. Maddox fixed them with his eye.

"Brenna," he said, holding out the book without releasing the couple from his gaze, "give this to Mr Hamilton, that he might never return to London."

Rafe was sweating, and shivering as if freezing. I hurried to Hamilton, who seemed himself transfixed by the couple's gaze.

"Take it and go," I said. "Quickly. And redeem yourself, if you can, in whatever way your religion deems right. For *his* sake," I added, indicating Rafe, "if for no other reason. He must believe it possible."

Hamilton nodded. "It's better this book leaves the world. Forever." Clasping the manuscript to him, he moved closer to the fire.

"One last thing," Rafe said, not turning his head. "Was it worth it, the suffering? To satisfy your curiosity? Your pride? To know…?"

The old man looked to me, then the hearth-stones. He made a strangled sound. "There was someone. Who died. She was … precious to me."

Rafe said nothing for a long moment. "And did you find her?"

Hamilton shook his head. "Not yet."

He took another step closer to the fire, nodded to me, and walked into the flames, springing instantly up the vast chimney.

At the doors, the couple inclined their perfect heads as if to bid Rafe *adieu*, or something else, until they should meet again. And they were gone.

Rafe remained, shaking. I guided him to one of the chairs by the hearth, and after searching in the dark corners of the room found a little *uisce* in a decanter, to calm him.

We sat while the logs burned low, and turned to embers, until at last Rafe seemed to return from wherever he had gone.

"Ζητηιν Ανακαλύπτειν Νοστέιν," said Rafe.

"Yes?"

"It's the motto, of the Etheric Explorers."

It had been a long time since I had heard any Greek spoken. "To … seek, to discover, to … return home?" I translated.

"The older I grow, Brenna, the more the final command speaks to me."

It was late, and soon I too would have to go back to another place. There was just a faint glow in the hearth when Rafe turned to me in the dim light and spoke again.

"Hamilton left in, what, 1830?" Rafe elbowed himself up from where he had sunken into the chair. "He knows nothing of photography."

I was about to reply that I knew nothing of it either, until I remembered his "slides". Now I worry for Rafe.

Part III

THE OBJECTS OF the Etheric Explorers Club's researches are not the only aspects of the society which are of interest; the members themselves are a source of innumerable curious anecdotes. Never ossifying into a mere professional association, the club has always drawn members from a richly assorted range of amateurs (in the best sense of the term). Quite early in its history, in the 1880s, it began accepting women into its ranks, eventually even admitting some living ones.

The very premises, too, are deserving of at least a passing mention. They were inherited by Dr Rafe Maddox from his cousin, Miss Bronwyn Griggs, the noted mathematician. Rather like Emmy Noether in a later generation (whose name, I need hardly say, has no connexion with the *ether* discussed here), Maddox's cousin was one of the few women working at the time in her field of mathematics and mathematical physics. Both were interested in fundamental questions, though of a somewhat different nature. Whereas Noether's Theorem raises interesting questions pertaining to the origin of the cosmos – that is, if the Lagrangian of physical systems in the early cosmos was not symmetric under translations in time or space as it is today, then momentum and energy need not have been conserved, accounting perhaps for why the matter in the universe exists at all, and why it continues to expand – Maddox's cousin Bronwyn's interests were directed towards the works of Bernhard Riemann in the fields of curved space and higher dimensions.

Since the earliest days, members have long been familiar with the curious resistance of their club premises to be quantified precisely. It is, for example, traditionally believed that the exact number of rooms varies from count to count, with no two persons agreeing on the figure. This indeterminacy has even extended to the number of floors on occasion. Accounts of members entering rooms only to apparently disappear, emerging later with no recollection of time having passed, are not uncommon.

Lest it should appear unduly coincidental, I must mention that the reason that the club's founder, Rafe Maddox, shares his name with the square upon which the club premises are located is that the family relationship between the Maddoxes and Miss Griggs planted the name in the minds of Rafe's parents. The legend that Dr Maddox was originally christened under a different name, but that his cousin's spirit contrived to change historical events by communicating somehow *backwards* in time is hardly credible, though a charming story.

Unimposing from without, the edifice has a number of other curious stories and legends associated with it, the most recent being perhaps one of the most dramatic: at the height of "the Blitz" a 1000 kg bomb was seen by a member of the fire brigade (of good and sober character) to plummet through the roof of the club, only to turn about-face and rocket skywards, where it collided with a Luftwaffe Heinkel He 111 bomber, destroying the aircraft in a stupendous explosion that brought down three other bombers flying in the same formation. Apart from minor damage to the roof and a few upper residential rooms, the premises escaped largely unscathed.

In common with the previous trio, it is from the founding generation that we get our final three tales, rather than from those involved in the upheavals of the early 20th century. It has been said of the members of the Etheric Explorers Club that they can frequently be found frustrating prophesies, wrestling with ancient evils, and generally striding boldly down the dark alleys of life in order to fill in those portions of man's map of reality that are, perhaps, better left blank. This is certainly true of "The Incident at the 27th Meeting", in which an experiment goes gravely wrong. Two of the society's eldest traditions trace their origins to the consequences of this incident, and it marks a turning point at which the club as a whole first acknowledged that their work carried with it serious responsibilities.

It may be said, too, of the affair related in "66° South", involving as it does a lost world which should perhaps have been left lost.

To this date, the region of Van Zinderman's Land in the Antarctic has never been fully explored. It has acquired an evil reputation amongst whalers, and no expedition on the scale of Kirkland's has since been mounted. Albert McAvoy's account, upon which "66° South" is grounded, was entrusted to the captain of the steamer that left him to hover on that dreadful shore. Whether he ever returned, I could not discover with certaintly. The only evidence that I could find lay in a letter from a visitor to Sarawak who had heard of a British man in that country supposedly brought there from the southern ocean on a sealing vessel enroute to China to sell a cargo of Weddell seal skins. He did not, or could not, speak, so nothing more of his story was known. Perhaps we will never know.

As with any club, though, there are always members who stay behind so as not to miss a second helping of pudding; we have their story in "The Resident Member", which in addition to this form has also been skillfully adapted and performed as a wireless drama by Digby Young, Joe Vaz, Gideon Emery, Damon Berry, and Christa Schamberger-Young, produced by *Something Wicked* magazine, and broadcasted by a number of stations in the Dominion of Canada and in the United States of America.

The Incident at the 27ᵗʰ Meeting

IT IS ONLY now, with the passing of Eustice Pillman, that I may with good conscience relate the awful events of the 27ᵗʰ meeting of the Etheric Explorers Club. Until that night we, the members, were what you might call tourists in the spirit realm, visiting for curiosities and amusements, but flitting in and out as a traveller might who merely wished to sample an exotic land, soon returning to his ship to move on to the next port. All of those present that night still walk in its shadows, much as we try to outrun them.

Of course, the purpose of our association is to seek out and reveal the hidden world of the spirit, and much of the matter of our investigations would appear fantastical or *outré* to the layman. Nevertheless, I believe it to be in the public's interest to be aware that these phenomena may sometimes intrude upon their experience, and indeed the common man must be prepared for the day when manifestations of the ephemeral world are as commonplace as the locomotive or the breech-loading cannon. Without such preparation, much misery may arise from the misuse of the knowledge that we have wrung so dearly from nature.

Being at that time a bachelor, I dined early after spending a pleasant afternoon translating papyri at the British Museum, and was the first to arrive at the club premises on St. Raphael's Square. First, but for Maddox, who was readying himself for his presentation to the members, for we took it in turns to deliver a lecture each week on some subject of interest. It struck me as peculiar that he had erected a curtain to obscure his preparations, but one assumed that it was somehow relevant, or that he desired to offer a dramatic revelation of some kind. Maddox, a young man at that time, had recently astounded his academic peers with his unprecedented refusal of the Lucasian Chair at Oxford, to "pursue Natural Philosophy unhindered by the prejudices of the foolish and the old," as he said. But such were his achievements in pure mathematics and the study of the electromotive forces that his reputation only grew by his strange refusal of the highest dignity of his profession.

Billingsly, the club footman, had piled the hearth high against the unhealthy damp cold of the night. However, the man had been stoking the fire with cheap lignite coal again, despite my expressed wishes that he buy a better grade. It was no doubt done from some perverse sense of economy, inspired by that dissenter chapel he attended. The fellow was constantly leaving pamphlets about the club library condemning the Church of England. He would have been sent packing back to his chapel had it not been for his past, but that is another matter. In any case, the chimney was not drawing well that night, and there was a disagreeably sulphurous atmosphere in the meeting hall.

Through one reason or another, only eight of the members attended. De Ramsey was present, but craved our indulgence if he were called away early, for he suspected that a vote of confidence might be called in the House that evening, and he had been obliged to keep the party whip informed of his whereabouts, lest the government fall from having too few members present. Thompson and Briscoe arrived together, having just dined out. They, and the rest, Hargrove, Jenkins, Pillman, and I settled into our accustomed places around the table as Billingsly brought in the sherry, pouring us each a glass, except for Hargrove, who in addition to being a Harley Street physician was also abstemious, and a vegetarian.

"You wouldn't touch the stuff if you had seen the livers and bowels I've seen on the post mortem slab," he would tell anyone who raised an eyebrow at his preferences. I daresay he is correct, but then dissection would put any sensible man off his dinner.

De Ramsey proposed the loyal toast, "To Her Majesty, the Queen," and we all raised our sherry glasses.

"What's the tinkerer got for us today then, eh?" asked Pillman, downing his glass and pouring another.

As was usual, he displayed impatience when faced with delay or complexity, being less captivated by theory and discovery than with matters relating to personal immortality, which I suspect was his sole interest in the club. A stockbroker by trade, Pillman was a corpulent man with the physiognomy of a prize-fighter gone to

fat, and he entertained himself by devising mildly insulting sobri-
quets for his friends and acquaintances. Maddox had been given
the name tinkerer owing to his love of devices. He peered over his
curtain.

"Just a few moments gentlemen," Maddox replied.

"I've been doing some interesting reading on the subject of the
prophesies of Nostradamus," Briscoe said.

"Damn Nostradamus," Thompson suggested. "The fellow's
about as clear as a coal miner's spectacles. It's a fool's game to try
to make anything out of his nonsense. I've been telling you so for
the past hour."

"I wonder, has anyone given any thought to the club motto I
suggested?" asked Jenkins.

"You know what you can do with your Greek mottoes, Alcibiades!" exclaimed Pillman, thinking this a very clever nick-name
for Jenkins, who though a student of Greek was as meek and unlike the military commander Alcibiades as could be imagined.

"A proper motto should be Latin," Hargrove stated, smacking
the table to defy any argument to the contrary.

I believe I drew his attention to the fact that heraldic conven-
tions allow mottoes in several languages, but Hargrove did not
welcome my contribution. Perhaps medical men do not appreciate
being reminded that their Greek knowledge is limited to the Oath
of Hippocrates and the Staff of Asclepius.

"Gentlemen," Maddox announced finally, "I am ready to
begin."

He emerged from behind the curtain and lifted up a corner to
wipe some fluid from his hands, dropping back the veil before any
of us could make out the hidden object.

"I believe you are all familiar with my theories of the morphology of the etheric organ, but there are certain points I would like to
reiterate in order to render the object of tonight's discussion more
comprehensible."

Brushing off his coat, he continued, "It is my conviction that
the mind, or soul if you prefer, is a process originating in the brain,
but potentially independent of it. Just as electric charges may pro-
duce oscillations in the ether, so may subtler undulations arise in
the conduits of the brain, creating complex overlapping patterns

of waves. These variations in the ether are generally localized within the skull, extending only slightly beyond the insulating layer of bone. And so, as the bulges and features of the cranium may be read by a trained phrenologist as a crude cerebral map, I would suggest that by detecting these mental waveforms we may peer more accurately into the dark regions of the mind. And this, gentlemen, is how I propose to do it!"

Maddox seized a rope and pulled away the curtain to expose his apparatus. We stared in silence, except for Hargrove, who grunted at the sight. Not being of a mechanical inclination, it would be difficult for me to accurately describe the machine, but my impression was of a large mahogany case with numerous knobs and buttons presumably serving some electrical function. Attached to these by a bundle of fine wires was a singular object, roughly the size of a pumpkin, but constructed of brass bands with what appeared to be translucent sausages on the inner surfaces.

Thompson nodded with an impressed look, but Hargrove waved contemptuously at the thing.

"Just what do you propose to discover with this, this absurd contraption that I can't find out with a pair of callipers and my two hands?"

"My dear Hargrove, the bumps of the phrenologist are mere symptoms. The waves contained within are the mind itself. By opening it to direct study, we may not only determine the features of the mind, but change them, reshape them for the better."

De Ramsey, until then preoccupied with some political intrigue or other, was the first to discern the importance of this.

"Good Lord, do you mean to say that your device can manipulate men's minds?"

Maddox smiled.

"Precisely. I expected that aspect to interest you, De Ramsey, given your work on the Penal Reform Committee. What I propose, gentlemen, is that many of the worst afflictions of mankind, such as madness, criminality, perhaps even evil itself, may be overcome using the science of the etheric organ."

We were dumbstruck, halfway between incredulity and amazement. Had such a claim come from anyone else, we would have greeted it as raving quackery, but Maddox was not a man to be dismissed lightly.

"I have only begun to tease out a few strands of the Gordian Knot of waves which constitutes consciousness. However, there have already been some successes, having identified, induced, and removed the impulses of greed and hunger in a test subject. I realize that you may harbour scepticism, and I applaud your critical faculties. Therefore I propose to demonstrate that the machine is effective on anyone willing to undergo the procedure."

We were indeed sceptical of the device, but of course such a challenge was irresistible to the Etheric Explorers, and there was a general willingness to give a fair test to the thing.

"Put Jenkins in the infernal device," suggested Pillman, with a bit of a sneer. "Five guineas says you can't find a nubbin of evil bone in his head!"

"Yes," agreed Hargrove. "But try to purge whatever imp it is that keeps him blithering on about Greek mottoes."

The challenge was accepted by Jenkins. We gathered about the apparatus whilst Maddox fitted the dome over Jenkins' head with some care, to orient it with precision.

"I regret that the fit may not be ideal, as it was previously configured for the cranium of a baboon," Maddox said apologetically. "The enclosure contains sacs of conductive jellies which respond to and amplify particular wavelengths, but which may also be used to influence and control the same waves. There, Jenkins, how does that feel?"

There was some indecipherable mumbling from within the helmet, but it seemed to nod approvingly, and so Maddox carried on.

"Now gentlemen, we have all recently had a good repast, and so there should be no need for any hunger in the room. I will attempt to induce a craving for food in Jenkins, and we will see what he has to say about his mental state following the experiment. Briscoe, would you lend a hand on that crank to charge the apparatus?"

As Briscoe powered the dynamos, a whirring buzz filled the hall as though a hive of bees had been installed. Maddox opened the side of his cabinet to perform some adjustment, giving me a brief view of a mass of wires and glass bathed in a faint orange glow, like the embers of a dying fire.

Maddox continued describing the procedure to us.

"The machine is now in a passive state, merely receiving impulses. Once the correct wave is isolated, there, yes, now the active functions may be engaged to begin influencing the subject."

Jenkins twitched slightly, perhaps trying to better hear what was being said.

"Are you experiencing any sensations?" shouted Maddox.

The mass of brass and jelly turned and nodded again, Jenkins pointing clumsily to where one presumes he thought his mouth was. Failing that, he pointed to his belly.

"By Jove, there really is something to this," Thompson exclaimed.

Maddox began making minor changes to the helmet's angle as we congratulated him on the apparent success of the thing, and he told Briscoe to cease powering the machine, as it had stored enough charge for the rest of the evening.

"What keeps these waves from simply dissipating?" wondered Thompson.

"I believe that they may collectively form what has been called a solitary wave, which is self-sustaining. Perhaps you are acquainted with Russell's work on solitary waves in canals? There are certain aspects of the problem that are connected, strangely enough, to astronomy as well. Have you read my paper on the Three Body Problem, published by the Royal Society? The instabilities are somewhat akin."

Pillman seemed unimpressed.

"I hardly see anything miraculous in making a fellow peckish," he observed, and fiddled with some the instruments on the cabinet, idly jabbing at buttons and twiddling knobs. "Why not do something a little more worthwhile for him?"

"Damn you, Pillman, stop messing about," Maddox began, pushing the fool away from the controls, but before he could say anything further we were all paralysed by the site of Jenkins thrashing his limbs about, desperately attempting to lurch out of his seat and tear the helmet from his head, muffled cries coming from inside the mass of metal and wires. Maddox worked his machine in a frenzy to undo the disorder, but to little effect. Long sickening moments passed until Pillman seized hold of Jenkins, tearing at the dome with his hands. They toppled over together, Jenkins limp as a doll and both of them covered from head to waist in jelly and wires. Pillman struggled feebly with the slippery tangle until we dragged the two men free of the mess, sitting them up for reviving brandy. Maddox was furious with the vandal.

"Get your wits about you and get out, Pillman, you're a bloody disgrace!" he told him.

After the careless fellow had departed in a cloud of shame, Maddox was abject in his expressions of regret to Jenkins.

"My dear fellow, I am so sorry. None of this was meant to happen! That imbecile Pillman was tampering with the device. I hope you can forgive me."

Jenkins was still drowsy and unsteady, but he dismissed the whole affair with a wave of his hand. Maddox took charge of the victim, the two of them departing in Maddox's carriage bound for Jenkins' home, where his wife could put him to bed for some rest, to soothe his nerves.

"Bloody glad I didn't try the thing," commented Hargrove, as we separated to return to our respective houses.

I could only agree with him, and suggested that it would be best if Pillman were given the cold shoulder and told to stay away until feelings had settled down, letting him have time to ponder his transgression.

Two days later I learnt in *The Times* of the inexplicable Regent's Park Horror. A gentleman had strangled his wife, and then gone on to savagely murder and mutilate his housemaid, finally doing away with himself. They found Jenkins' body hanging from a chandelier. The news struck us all hard, but especially Maddox, who was sick with grief from his mistaken sense of responsibility. He speculated that Pillman's meddling had somehow induced the complete inversion of what he called Jenkins' "primary moral harmonic", but the explanation did little to dispel the gloom that shrouded our hearts. There was no debate when I mooted a motion to blackball Pillman and expel him permanently from the club, nor any argument when Hargrove suggested adopting Jenkins' motto.

Some months later I happened by chance to encounter Eustice Pillman in the street. At first I barely recognized the fellow, for so pitiably transformed was he that his face was almost that of another man. He stuttered out an awkward confession of remorse, but appeared too broken in spirit to pull himself together. I was not a terribly sympathetic listener, making a weak excuse to leave him as quickly as I could. Apparently his regret was sincere, for soon after our meeting he abandoned the stock market, using his savings to found a hospital near the headwaters of the Nile, labouring there for his sins. Always a selfish, indulgent man when I knew him, it is somehow pathetic that he would attain a sympathetic conscience only to be condemned by it to an unrelieved misery of regret. The news reached me only this morning that he has perished of fever, there in the barbarous land of his penitence.

The incident might have destroyed our society, but instead we chose to continue the meetings of the Etheric Explorers Club, with time proving that, in the balance, more triumph than tragedy was to come of our work. Now each meeting is held beneath the sobering gaze of Jenkins' portrait, commissioned by the club and hung in our meeting hall. It hangs beside others who have been lost along our journey, to remind those remaining of the costs of knowledge, and of carelessness, when exploring deep in the unknown.

66° South

I ADMIT THAT WHEN I invited Jonathan Kirkland to lecture us concerning his travels in the Antarctic Seas it was not so much for their relevance to the Etheric Explorers Club, nor to my own passion for ancient ruins, but partly as a revenge upon Perkins. Perkins had, the previous week, inflicted upon us the company of a dubious Hindoo Yogi of some renown. As it turned out, this person was actually a native of Aberdeen who was in the habit of wearing a loin-cloth and darkening his skin with a preparation of walnut husks. While Kirkland was certainly no such charlatan, he did have a reputation for possessing a nigh inexhaustible repertoire of nautical anecdotes, which I knew to be the type of tale that Perkins found particularly irksome. Moreover, Kirkland was an old school-mate of mine, and though in the intervening years we had fallen out of touch, nevertheless I thought we might yet have the bond of the old *alma mater*.

In the twenty-odd years since I had last seen him, Kirkland had certainly been weathered by time. His great beak of a nose was instantly recognizable, though it now adorned a countenance that the savagery of nature had left ruddy and furrowed. His pale blue eyes were the same as well, though strangely cold now, with a distant horizon always within them. He seemed to have diminished in stature, but it was merely a slight slouching of the shoulders that gave this impression, as though he were still leaning into the harness of a heavily-laden sledge. We shook hands as he entered the club library. It was a momentary shock to realize that he was missing three finger tips on his right hand, and he must have seen it in my face.

"Lost them to frostbite," he explained. "Good to see you again, McAvoy," he added.

"And you, old man. What a time you must have had out there.

We're all eager to hear of it."

Kirkland nodded. Apart from the official account of the expedition, which had been published earlier in the year, he had not spoken in public of it. That we should be the first outsiders to hear of it from his own lips was a boon I was keenly sensible of, but I put the favour down to our old acquaintance.

We took chairs at the long ebony table in the library, and once such of the membership as were attending had seated themselves, I rose to offer the toast to the Queen, and introduced our speaker.

"Gentlemen, you are acquainted by reputation with our guest, and are no doubt familiar with many of the events of his travels through newspaper accounts and the chatter of society, but tonight we have the privilege to hear his story at first hand; tomorrow we shall be boasting of our luck to the disappointed members of the Royal Geographic Society. I give you Mr Jonathan Kirkland."

At the head of the table, Kirkland stood to address us with the posture of one gazing off a deck, pipe in hand and feet apart.

"My first attraction to the Southern Continent arose when, as a boy, I was given by an uncle a small stone said to have been found on an iceberg near the Antarctic coast. Since that time, I longed to see the home of that stone with my own eyes. From this beginning, gentlemen, came our mission: to chart an unknown coastal region of the Antarctic, as well as to map any accessible mountain ranges in the vicinity. I christened the region Van Zinderman's Land after the captain of a Dutch expedition, the only others ever to visit the place, though sadly they never returned. Once partial financing was secured, we purchased *The Nunutak*, a 240-ton steam-whaler with three masts and a 120 horsepower engine. Shearing, my first officer, assembled a crew ..."

Across the table, Perkins was growing visibly discomfited with the maritime jargon, but I took little satisfaction from it, as Kirkland's tale was proving to be too engrossing to permit distraction. He described his journey southward, first to Montevideo for provisions and repairs, thence to the Falklands, 'round the Horn, and into the bleak Antarctic waters that lie along 66° south latitude, between the longitudes of Hawaii and Capetown. At Beatrix Island, within sight of a small bay on the opposite shore, they established a base. Leaving Mr Shearing in command of the lifeless pile of rock, Kirkland crossed the strait and made landfall upon the continent.

"Our party went ashore to assemble the huts, unload the dogs and supplies, and scout the area. I say ashore, but no exposed land presented itself apart from a narrow shingle entirely carpeted with Weddell seals and penguins making an overpowering din and stench. We were forced to make camp atop the thousand-mile-long wall of ice that towered over the coast like the cliffs of Dover. Several crewmen remained on the beach to slaughter such animals as were needed for winter food and fuel, and for oil to offset the substantial cost of the expedition. I regretted the killing, for they are gentle, curious creatures, and it tainted our mission to spill their blood. Nevertheless, it was necessary. But finding it distasteful, I left with the team ascending the glacier."

Their new station was built right upon the Antarctic circle and it seemed an admirable location, for it lay adjacent to an unmapped mountain chain bearing at least two active volcanoes. Kirkland had been struck by the splendour of the peaks, naming the range for Samantha, the wife he had married just weeks before his departure. The fauna thereabouts were as little known as the geography, and in the empty quarter of ice beyond the coast the wandering magnetic pole was thought to dwell, its current position a mystery.

They had arrived during the short summer, when temperatures hovered near 32°F, and the pack ice was blown out to sea, allowing ships to approach. Planning to overwinter with the well-anchored *Nunutak* frozen into the pack, they would travel overland to explore the Samanthian Mountains, while at the base camp others gathered meteorological data and observed the polar lights. Waterspouts were often seen near their base, and a great deal was learnt of the peculiar weather in those parts, with a record wind velocity of 191 mph measured shortly before their anemometer was blasted to bits.

When his description of the expedition finished, with all of its remarkable phenomena and anecdotes of hardship, there was a burst of sincere applause that Kirkland received with thoughtful dismissal. Afterwards, as the little group of members dissipated towards the door to collect hats and coats, Kirkland drew me aside and addressed me in undertones.

"There's another matter I need to discuss," he said, glancing about at the diminishing audience. "I understand your club has some … experience of these things. I should like your counsel, and that of any of your colleagues whose discretion you trust."

I could not imagine what he was hinting at, but I caught the eye of Rafe Maddox and beckoned him over to us.

"Would you mind joining us in the smoking room, Maddox? Our guest seeks advice."

By shutting ourselves in we signalled other members not to disturb us, since otherwise the smoking room was always left open. Maddox knelt to light the fire that was laid in the hearth, while Kirkland and I took armchairs nearby. With a raised eye-brow Maddox wondered what it was all about. Pursed lips and a slight shrug told him I knew no more than he.

Reclining, Kirkland lit his pipe with the habitual hand-cupping of one used to fending off katabatic gales. Maddox watched, and leant against the mantelpiece.

"Your crew did some fine work on the magnetic pole, and the aurora," he commented.

Nodding at the compliment, Kirkland puffed to kindle his to-bacco.

"It's not scientific matters I seek your advice about. Though surely you're as adept in that field as in this."

We waited. Evidently Kirkland was reticent to discuss the mat-ter. Perhaps he had long borne the weight of it alone, in silence. He fidgeted with his watch fob, and a rattling was coming from his gnashed pipe-stem. When he had composed himself, he continued.

"There were episodes in the expedition which none of the crew have spoken of. Episodes for which I have no adequate explana-tion."

"Go on, old man," I encouraged him. "You may rely on Mad-dox and me to keep to ourselves anything you wish to relate."

"It began the very day we arrived. With the completion of the huts atop the glacier, we rejoined the sealing party on the beach. I expected a repugnant scene, for a place of wholesale slaughter is never pleasant. What we saw, though … I've seen men kill before: some grimly; some efficiently; but God help me, I had never be-fore beheld a group of men in such a blood-lust. The beach was slick with gore, and the bay was red with it. They had killed ten times what we needed. And they were *laughing* all the while. Even as we arrived, one man, as if for a joke, drove his pickaxe though his companion's chest. The wretched fellow dropped dead at once. They all stopped their antics then."

I exchanged glances with Maddox, who was as astonished as I. Kirkland was shaking his head in dismay at his recollections.

"Sorenson, a Swede who'd taken ship with us, did the murder. It was a foul business. Needless to say, there was no court out there. As captain, I passed the sentence, and he was hanged, still foul with blood.

Maddox cleared his throat. "I recall mention of casualties on the expedition. None of murder," he observed.

"In light of subsequent events, it was agreed that the deaths would be called accidents, to spare the families any grief or shame."

With this revelation I began to sense the gravity of Kirkland's burden. "It must have cast a pall over the rest of the expedition," I speculated.

"More than the twenty-hour nights of June. But that was merely our welcome to Van Zinderman's Land. Morale eroded day by day. Grim thoughts come naturally in such places, with work the only remedy. At first our little feasts — birthdays, anniversaries, and the like — relieved the strain, but gradually the tension grew. Men accused one another of theft. We bickered over unequal rations and work loads. There was a rumour in the glacier huts that the island team was sneaking rum from the ship. Shearing and I did our best to suppress it, but a coolness had developed between us which made resolution difficult.

"As we were ice-locked 'til December, I deemed it wisest to follow our original schedule. Consequently I led a party to the mountains consisting of Ferrier the meteorologist, John Walters, and Jones the palaeontologist. We took two months' supplies on two sledges, led by our best dogs, Job and Roma. More food had been cached near the mountains by an advance party.

"A crevasse-ridden ice field was our first obstacle. Harrowing as it was, it would have been unmemorable except for a singular meeting in the midst of that white desert. Four days from base, a lone Weddell seal crossed our path, heading inland. It was such a strange place to find the creature, we hastened to it, not knowing why it traversed the foodless interior. We attempted to turn it, thinking it confused or lost, but the beast merely stared at us with its watery black eyes and set off again towards the pole, and to its certain death. There was much discussion of it in the tents at night until the talk turned morbid, and I forbade any further mention of the event."

Kirkland paused to refill his pipe.

"Certainly an odd occurrence," I agreed.

"Perhaps the creatures are misled somehow by the proximity to the magnetic pole," Maddox suggested.

With a gesture Kirkland indicated he had pondered many explanations without satisfaction. "Whatever the case, we proceeded to the Samanthians, where we threaded our way back and forth between the peaks, gathering minerals and fossils. Jones found some ammonites which particularly excited his attention. One dog weakened, and was fed to the others. Ferrier was upset at this, being kind-hearted, but he was assuaged, or distracted, by the curious weather. So dry and windy was it that at night a pale glow could be seen around the stones where the air charged them with electricity.

"After twelve weeks we found ourselves in a position to spy a black column rising from the ship. How long the engines had been fired up, or why, we had no idea, but as the mission was nearly complete we turned back at once, dreading some disaster.

"Jones urged caution lest we plunge headlong into a fathomless crack in the ice, but I insisted it was essential to return quickly in case the ship, our only means of escape, was in danger. Perhaps my judgement is to blame for what followed. Within a day's march of camp we were sledging abreast when a snowlid collapsed, plunging both sledges into a crevasse. Ferrier and I were with one sleigh, which crashed into a ledge, crushing all of the dogs but Roma. Walters, Jones, and the other sledge were nowhere to be seen. In any event, we were in no position to help them, for we went glissading down a slope at ever increasing speed, tangled in a jumble of dead or dying dogs and smashed equipment.

"I have no idea how long the descent lasted. It seemed alternately like a second or an age. The light faded from blue to black as we slid, but eventually our rate of fall subsided with the gradient, and we found ourselves sprawled upon solid earth. Groping amongst the wreckage I located a lantern. I freed Roma from her traces and examined our tomb, feeling certain escape was impossible. Our crampons were on the other sledge. Without them there was no way to ascend the slope. Shouting for Jones and Walters produced no reply. Ferrier was concussed from the crash and half insensible.

"Evidently the glacier was shifting, for the walls shuddered intermittently. Bangs like rifle shots came out of the ice, and a constant rain of shattered crystals struck us from overhead. Taking what supplies we could, we probed passages through the glacier, threading past an outcrop of rock until a cavern opened before us. The dark space yielded nothing to our eyes at first. Suddenly the lantern illuminated something. There were signs of habitation."

Pausing, Kirkland fiddled again with his watch chain, making me wonder what the grey fob was. It resembled a musket ball.

"The Dutch expedition?" Maddox asked.

"Bones. Human bones. A seam of green copper lay embedded in the ground too, which I took at first to be a natural deposit. It was too straight and regular, however. As we followed it through the dark chamber, signs appeared on the metal at intervals. Strange, foreign marks. Like hieroglyphs, perhaps, though I know little of such things. It ended at a massive structure of stone, all seamlessly fitted without mortar. As to its purpose, I could tell nothing. All but the foundation was lost in the upper darkness. More bones littered the ground thereabouts. Nearby, we found and mounted broad steps to a platform or step pyramid of some kind on which lay a vast field of remains. Only then did I recognize that the damage to the skulls — holes punched through the temples — was not mere random ageing or accident, but the handiwork of some butcher, for amongst the bones I found a discarded tomahawk or warhammer with a cruel spike on one side. The same writing was evident on the bronze weapon, and carven in high relief into the stones of the dais.

"Before I could appreciate the enormity of the discovery, Jones' voice came echoing out of the blackness. Then his lantern appeared. Job, snarling, accompanied him as he rushed at us, wild with anger. Apparently Walters' neck had broken when he fell, and Jones was ravingly furious, blaming me for the catastrophe. Hardly of my own volition I lashed out with the warhammer, striking Jones' fist. He let out a howl, and the world seemed to go mad. An immense crash sounded. Roma leapt at Jones' throat. There was a ringing in my ears. Waves of sick pain washed over me. Jones lay dead, the dogs fighting over him. The roof was coming down upon us. I seized the stunned Ferrier and scrambled away, still clutching the lantern and warhammer in my free hand. Some providence led us to a channel cut by meltwater. We scrambled through fissures until at last daylight could again be seen filtering through the wall of the glacier. A mere crack led out, which I opened up by hacking at the ice. My grip was lost for an instant and the warhammer spun away into a crevasse, but we were able to squeeze through into the outside air, where we found ourselves above a beach with the sea in the distance beyond the pack ice.

"It was two day's march along the shore to find our base. That's when I lost these fingers. We arrived to find *The Nunutak* under siege. Shearing was aboard with his group. They were ramming her into the pack, trying to break out to open water. Around them, in a wide circle, were the rest of the crew, wielding axes or rifles. Fortunately my arrival caused such surprise that the civil war was briefly forgotten. I made the best of my opportunity by boarding the ship and assuming command. It was questionable whether peace could be maintained, but as the besiegers gathered 'round to join us or assault us I shouted for all to hear, that some malign influence was driving us mad, and that we must all escape the place together or perish there. Perhaps the horror of what was happening struck them suddenly, but they rushed onto *The Nunutak*. I set them all to tasks, hoping the united effort would prevent further fratricide. The sails were set and trimmed. The stokers kept the screws turning. Ahead, a party carried charges to blast a passage through the pack ice. The last of the coal went into the firebox, and with only a little progress made I was ready to despair, that the boiler would lose steam, that we would descend into murder and oblivion one final time. But Shearing took hold of my arm and said 'The oil. The carcasses!'. At once I ordered every man to haul our stores of blubber, penguins, and oil to the boiler room. It was all crammed into the blaze. Great strips of blubber, whole frozen penguins. The bones wicked up the oil, and the screws kept turning. At last we broke free of the ice, exhausted, our profits burnt to ash, but alive. All but for the eleven killed in various ways."

Maddox and I exchanged glances, but found nothing to say. Setting aside his pipe, Kirkland finished his tale.

"You may believe my account or not, gentlemen. I trust that you will at least not repeat it. I would, however, be grateful if you could make sense of it for me. For my part, the instant that continent slipped beneath the horizon in our wake, I vowed never to return to it, no matter how great my curiosity. Reunion with my beloved Samantha has only deepened my resolve in this."

"Is that the stone?" I asked, pointing at his watch-chain.

"This? Why yes, it's the stone I got as a lad."

He unclipped it from the chain and passed it to me.

"Take it, if you think it will teach you anything of this business. I need no mementoes of that cursèd place."

Obviously in a state of excitement, Maddox paced to and fro, rattling off half-finished sentences in speculation about the meaning of the tale. Kirkland just seemed relieved that we were not scoffing at him. Eventually, Maddox's hypotheses coalesced around a single focus. He believed that the ocean currents had once brought warmth to Van Zinderman's Land, much as the Gulf Stream does to Europe today. With the conditions far more temperate than at present, some ancient race, perhaps Polynesians or other sea-farers, had long ago settled there. Some terrible sacrificial religion had been practised, the evidence of which Kirkland had stumbled upon. Obviously some heat source — a hot spring perhaps — had prevented the ice from entirely enveloping the site.

More adventurously, Maddox mooted the notion that these ancients had employed mills or devices to gather electric current, sending it along the copper electroducts for some unguessed purpose. Or not unguessed, for Maddox ventured to suggest that they were able to manipulate the climate or the magnetic pole, even so far as to use it as a weapon against whatever unfortunate enemy from whom they had captured their sacrificial victims. Perhaps even at the moment of their overthrow they used their machines to sabotage the ocean currents, burying themselves and their enemies together forever in the ice.

Somehow their vicious conflict had survived their civilization, remaining in the land like a poison. There was not much else we could tell Kirkland to explain the tragedy, except that he was not mad, nor to blame. This seemed to be enough.

I learnt little from Kirkland's stone, but much from his story. I knew that such a singular opportunity for discovery would not come again in one lifetime, and so set about at once to arrange my passage to Van Zinderman's Land. Knowing Kirkland's experience, it was obvious that no group could long survive on that shore before each turned against each. That is how I find myself now steaming south in a whaler bound for Kerguelen Island. They have agreed to deposit me onto the Antarctic coast with equipment and supplies for two years, after which they will retrieve me. Alone, I will not be troubled by unwittingly murderous companions, and may discover the secret of that appalling shore. I only pray that I may remain sane long enough to come home with the truth. Nothing but a return to Van Zinderman's Land will shed any light on this affair. I confess though, that the lone seal troubles me.

The Resident Member

MONSIEUR BENOÎT, WHO was then the *chef de cuisine* at the Etheric Explorers Club, had, in an uncharacteristic mood of economy, merged the first two courses of our dinner into a quite exceptional bouillabaisse. Considering that only five members were present in the club on that Friday evening — a number further diminished when McCavour retired to his room upstairs long before dinner was served — I reminded myself to congratulate Benoît on his efforts. Even at the best of times these French chefs can be volatile artists, and I could well imagine his vexation at putting such effort into a dish for only four.

"Damn fine soup, eh Lichfield?" Cuthbertson asked me. "Bit like Mulligatawny," he added, and seemed to roll this idea about his mind for a time. "Only fishier," he decided.

As one of those leathery, heavily moustachioed Anglo-Indians, it still amazed me that Cuthbertson should end up with us, rather than at Boodle's, or the Savage Club, but I gather he met up with some Theosophists in the East, or some similar creatures, so I suppose that explains it. Whatever the case, I sincerely prayed that Benoît would never hear of his bouillabaisse having been described in the language that Cuthbertson had just used. Suppressing a shudder at the thought of our chef giving his notice, relegating us to the era of Lancashire hotpot as prepared by the club manservant, Billingsly, I humphed non-committally. It was only because there were too few of us to fill the dining room that night that we were forced to endure each other's company at all. But it seemed inhospitable to scatter ourselves at separate tables.

"I say," Milford piped up, "has anyone else ever tried swellfish?"

"What?" Cuthbertson asked, startled from his Mulligatawny reveries.

"Swell-fish." Milford repeated. "It's a fish," he explained.

As we waited for him to expand upon his chosen topic, I chewed another portion of *rouille*-seasoned bread.

"It swells up," he continued, "when it's alarmed. Like a bladder."

This image of Milford's gave us all, I think, pause for reflection. Selkirk, keeping to himself, merely winced at every new contribution to the discussion, unless he was responding to the garlic in the *rouille*. Cuthbertson set down his spoon.

"What the devil do you mean? My bladder doesn't swell up when it's alarmed!"

Milford seemed to grow abstract at this objection, staring off into the middle distance. "They call it *fugu* in Japan, of course," he said. "Should the fish be prepared in the wrong manner, the poison of the internal organs can mix with the flesh. Any diner unfortunate enough to consume such an ill-prepared dish suffers total and irreversible paralysis, while remaining completely and horribly conscious, in a nightmare-like living death. Finally, asphyxiation overcomes him, and he mercifully succumbs to oblivion."

Cuthbertson's moustache trembled slightly, and he pushed away his fish soup.

"Damn fool thing to do, if you ask me. Eating poison bladder-fish. Nonsense. What do you want to do a thing like that for?"

After spooning up some more broth, Milford considered the question. "Always interesting to try new things, I suppose."

"Madness," said Cuthbertson. He took a swig of the Provençal rosé that Benoît had imported specially, from Tavel. "Had elephant once m'self," Cuthbertson said. "Bit tough. Trunk's the best bit. Like veal. What about you, Lichfield? Ever eaten any odd-ball stuff?"

While I cannot claim to have supped on the exotica of the East, there was one thing that rose to the surface of a lifetime of memorable meals. "You know, I think the strangest thing I ever ingested was something I had once in Glasgow. A fellow there sold me a deep-fried pickle. Never had anything like it. Quite extraordinary."

Having finally lit upon a common area of interest, we were all now leaning back in our chairs with our glasses, recollecting meals gone by. Milford, again, was going on about some monstrous fruit from the Indies that smelt like an old boot and tasted of sherry custard.

"Ye gods," Cuthbertson broke in, "your palate belongs in Bedlam, Milford." He shook his head at the thought of the other fellow's lunatic indulgences, and then turned on Selkirk, who was sitting aloof, sniffing his rosé. "And what about you, Selkirk? Tell me your greatest ever tiffin wasn't some Chinese stink-berry."

"Wasn't Chinese," Milford protested feebly, before Cuthbertson waved him into silence. "Give Selkirk a chance," he insisted.

"Yes," I agreed, "I'd be fascinated to know, Selkirk."

Selkirk returned my gaze with his usual half-squint. He rubbed his chin, apparently sorting though his own culinary adventures. "Well, do you remember Peterson?"

"Peterson?" Milford asked.

"Yes," I muttered, the name coming back to me now. "Entomologist or something, wasn't he? Went out on your South American trek, up the Amazon?"

Selkirk nodded, gravely.

"Peterson died out there, if I remember correctly," I said.

A strange pallor fell over Milford's silent face. Cuthbertson's moustache twitched. "You don't mean to suggest…" he began, breathily, when Selkirk failed to elaborate.

"Surely…" said Milford.

Selkirk nodded again, in the same sad way.

"It's true," he admitted. "Disgusting, I know. I wouldn't want to make a habit of it, of course."

"Dear God," Cuthbertson said, retreating from Selkirk as far as possible without actually moving his chair.

Selkirk let out a long, world-weary sigh. "Yes. Yes, indeed. Makes you think, doesn't it. Poor fellow. The flesh had a nutty flavour, as I recall. Not bad at all, though, really. Cooked up quite nicely. Shame he never had a chance to add the grubs to his collection, but as a snack they weren't half bad."

As the waiter arrived bearing cutlets and claret, I sensed a certain loss of appetite in a couple of my companions, even if their colour was coming back. Just after the waiter had slipped away again, a heavy thump, as of a door slamming, sounded somewhere above us, causing a gilt gasolier in the centre of the dining room —

fashioned in the shape of five sinuous fire-breathing dragons — to sway gently, casting shifting shadows.

"McCavour must be tiring of our banter," I suggested.

"Fool's missing some good nosh," Cuthbertson opined, spreading butter on a slab of still-steaming bread. "What's he do with his time up there, anyway?"

Milford turned on his cutlet with such concentration that we knew he must be hiding something.

"Well?" Cuthbertson demanded. "What's he up to?"

Contorting his face like a man biting an unexpected olive stone, Milford lowered his voice. "He's a bit embarrassed just at present, I've heard."

"Embarrassed?" Cuthbertson exclaimed, far louder than even his normal boom. "'bout what? Hasn't got some filthy disease, has he? Knew a fellah in Rangoon, got a filthy disease. Auchenleck was the name. The fellah, not the disease."

I cleared my throat. "Impecunious, Milford means."

"Eh?" Cuthbertson said, looking from one to the other of us.

Milford's mouth dropped open and just as quickly swung itself shut again, as he evidently hunted for a polite synonym or euphemism. Selkirk abandoned his dinner and sat back, arms folded, shaking his head.

"What?" Cuthbertson demanded. His face umbered a trifle, as though basking in the heat of an over-banked moustache. He seemed to grow suddenly palsied in his annoyance, his fork shivering in his fist. But then it shook itself free and shot upward like a dart, burying itself in the high moulded ceiling.

"I say!" said Milford.

"What'n blazes!" exclaimed Cuthbertson.

"That's odd," I observed.

Even Selkirk rallied from his funk to join us in gawping up at the implement embedded overhead.

"I say," Milford repeated, tilting his head for a better look at the phenomenon.

Suddenly the evening was looking more promising. "Magnetism, do you think?" I asked.

Selkirk seized his spoon and squinted at it. "Sterling," he declared.

"Hm."

We all inspected our dining instruments, trying to give the impression that we could interpret the mysterious hallmarks stamped into the silver. This procedure, however, failed to shed any light on the behaviour we had witnessed. As we mused about it, Milford's knife was the next to shrug off Newton's inverse-square law and become airborne, but instead of flying heavenward it hovered a foot or so above his plate, trembled, and then darted over to within an inch of his throat. Milford squeaked in alarm, though the blade made no further attempt to transfix him. Instead, it wobbled in a seemingly annoyed manner, then rocketed into the ceiling to join its fellow.

"I say," breathed Milford, with real feeling this time.

But before we had the opportunity to delve into this latest occurrence, the remaining cutlery upended itself, danced about frenziedly over the table, and then hurtled headlong after the knife . A considerable quantity of plaster descended as a result, dusting the cutlets, plates, claret, and to some extent, us.

"I believe, gentlemen," I said, shaking out my napkin and dusting myself off with it, "that I have eaten sufficient for one evening." Eying the wayward cutlery, I edged back from the table in case gravity was about to re-assert its dominion. The others followed suit, deplastering themselves as best they could.

"Bloody McCavour," grumbled Cuthbertson. "Suppose he's up there summoning daemons."

"More like the ghost of Hans Christian Ørsted," Milford suggested.

"It's *not magnetism*," Selkirk was assuring us, when presently the gasolier began acting oddly as well. It waxed and waned in hypnotising pulses of light, joined in a moment when the rest of the gaslights in the room started throbbing in waves from the entrance hall to the main staircase. Selkirk glared at the gas-jets like a predator. Cuthbertson picked peevishly at the plaster shards dissolving in his claret.

"Don't you think it's a bit of a stretch to picture McCavour mixed up in all that Faust and devils business?" I said. "I've always had him down as more of an astrology and patent-medicines man. Anyhow, surely there's some club rule against doing anything, you know, of an occult or apocalyptic nature, while staying in club lodgings."

To be perfectly candid, however, the dining room at least was becoming decidedly daemonic, what with the pulsing flames and the menacingly animated silverware. Milford seemed to be particularly affected. Reasonably so, I'm sure, given the bounderly behaviour of his knife.

"I think I'll, I'll just …" he said, pulling out his watch for a meaningful look.

"No, no," I declared, giving him a re-assuring, if dusty, pat on the back, "What would Doctor Maddox and the rest of our society's dauntless, but absent, vanguard say if we should fly at the first inklings of a diabolical presence? Let us see if we can get to the bottom of these unnatural goings-on."

Having thus obtained a semblance of agreement — grudging from Milford, steadfast from Selkirk, and somewhat indifferent from Cuthbertson — we proceeded through the Stygian illumination towards the main stairs, to find and interview McCavour. On the way we encountered our waiter who, perhaps because of our wraithlike dusting, stopped dead upon catching sight of us. Or it may be that he was wondering how we had worked sixteen pieces of cutlery into a fifteen-foot-high ceiling. We shall never know, for the waiter, in spite of his doubtless fine qualities — uncorking bottles, polishing utensils, folding napkins, and the like — had no stomach for our enterprise. We must bid him adieu, and good fortune wherever he next seeks employ. He shall enter our tale, and our club, no further.

"Milksop," Cuthbertson muttered after the retreating waiter.

Before mounting the stairs we paused beside the vast bearded Pythagoras, in marble, which forms the main baluster. As the stone Greek glared at his triangle, so did we ponder Selkirk, with puzzlement. He was blocking the stairs; evidently to some purpose, as he had produced some string from his pocket and was deftly tying something up like a tiny parcel.

"Sixpence," he explained, as if this were an explanation.

We were daunted neither by the sinister forces awaiting us on the first floor, nor even by Selkirk's occult string-tricks, and so we ascended the stairs with no more than the amount of caution that would be expected under the circumstances. Selkirk took the lead, stalking slowly upward while holding out his wobbling sixpence, looking like a carriage harnessed to a fly.

Half-way up the gently-curving staircase a second, louder, thump came from the floor above. Cuthbertson stopped, and riffled through his pockets. I looked at him quizzically.

"Are you going to try half a crown and some jute twine?" I inquired.

"Damn it, I've lost m'Dutch cigars," he said, before locating the objects. Cuthbertson drew one out and lit it.

"Why," I asked, turning again toward Selkirk, "are we following a sixpence?"

Sighing like a Latin Master after his hundredth repetition of a basic declension, Selkirk held out his dangly thingummy.

"Do you know what this is?" he demanded.

"If I am not very much deceived, it is a sixpence."

"A *silver* sixpence. The phenomenon clearly has an affinity for silver, ergo I am using silver to detect its presence. There. Can you all understand that?"

Milford was affronted, but I nodded genially enough, considering Selkirk's churlish tone.

"What?" inquired Cuthbertson. He had been leaning over the banister, dropping spent matches into a potted aspidistra some distance below.

"Oh, for God's sake," Selkirk said, skulking off again with his coin.

"Did you just happen to have some string?" I asked him as we ascended. A stern face turned to me, as if I'd inquired of an infantryman to which end of a rifle one was meant to attach the bayonet.

"*Always* carry string, Lichfield," he admonished.

Vowing to live by this commandment, I followed valiant Selkirk onto the landing, where the only apparent untoward activity was some wavering in the gaslights. Selkirk swivelled carefully this way and that, peering down the corridors to right and left. Incredibly, the walls appeared to be covered in green baize, but this can be blamed on the fact that they were. I did not wish to interfere with Selkirk's delicate observations, and so restrained myself from toddling immediately down to McCavour's room, to the right. While I held back, Milford edged over and muttered in my ear.

"There's always been … something. Something upsetting about these upstairs rooms. I don't know. A presence. They've always disturbed me."

"My dear fellow," I said, "courage. It's the décor that does it. I feel the same way, I assure you."

"This way," Selkirk ordered, and led us along the leftward corridor. He lifted the sixpence to each door as we passed, as though checking the numbers with a lantern. After testing six rooms, we arrived at the long mirror at the dead end of the hall.

"Sixpence!" snorted Cuthbertson. He puffed a defiant smoke ring at Selkirk. Meanwhile, I availed myself of the opportunity to straighten my collar in the looking glass, and to remove a little more plaster from my nose. I started, thinking I had seen …something. But then the glass fogged over.

"Stand back!" warned Selkirk. He reached out to the misty glass with a barely trembling hand to touch it for an instant. "Cold," he declared. "Ice cold. And silvered," he added, meaningfully.

We hardly knew what to make of it when, as if an unseen finger were touching the glass, a dot was cleared of mist. It stretched into a long, graceful curve that seemed to be forming a circle until it pinched in slightly on the left side.

"It's a … what is it?" Cuthbertson asked.

Selkirk, assuming that we relied upon his authority in such matters, scrutinized the figure carefully. He held his sixpence up to it before forming his conclusions.

"It is a persimmon," he declared.

"Is it?" I asked, feeling certain nameless doubts.

Milford tipped his head on one side for a better look at the drawing. "It *is* rather like a persimmon. A tipped-over persimmon."

"You don't suppose," I mused, "that it could be a cardioid?"

"Eh?" said Cuthbertson.

"A figure," I explained, "which mathematicians make using x, y, cosines, radii, and squiggles of that sort. Introduced in *The Philosophical Transactions of the Royal Society*, circa 1741 if I recall rightly, by Giovanni Francesco Salvemini, also known as

Johann Castillon."

The others stared with an incredulity that was slightly offensive.

"You *amaze* me, Lichfield," Selkirk said eventually, in another of his tones. "Can you *really* not see that it's a persimmon? After all that nonsense you lot were spouting about Scottish fried pickles and Chinese stink-berries, obviously the spirit has been stimulated to tell us about eating persimmons. Honestly, Lichfield. I expected more from you."

"They aren't Chinese," Milford protested, though no-one was listening.

Our attentions were turned to the glass again when more drawing began beneath the figure. Letters this time.

"G...O..." Selkirk read out, "G O B A C K."

"Perhaps it would like us to go back to McCavour's room," I suggested. "It's back the way we came, down the other corridor."

As no reply came to my knocks, Cuthbertson stepped forward to wale against door with his balled fist. "Wake up, McCavour, you great suet pudding," he hollered, in case his pounding was insufficient to do the job. When there was still no stirring, Cuthbertson tried the knob and went in.

McCavour was there, sure enough; we found him fallen, face down on the rug, along with a ponderous brass planter that had tipped over. We hastened to turn him right side up, but from the moment we saw his purplish jowls, and the way his eyes were starting from out of his doughy face, we knew it was all up for McCavour. Selkirk checked for a pulse to confirm McCavour's doom.

"Dead," he decreed. "Dead as an aurochs."

With some significant effort, and considerable argument, we shifted McCavour's corpse to his bed, and then stood about it respectfully.

"Poor fellow," said Milford. "Must have had a weak heart. Ought we to send for an undertaker?"

Cuthbertson stroked his chin. "S'pose we'll need to summon a sawbones to sign the death warrant, or whatever it's called."

"Certificate?" I suggested. I noticed Selkirk was wincing again. "What's the club policy for this sort of thing?" I asked. The others considered the question, but were only vaguely aware of the existence of such a thing as the club rule book.

"Ring for Billingsly," said Milford. "He'll know what to do with a body."

I tugged the bell rope. An instant later, Billingsly stumbled through the door as though shoved on stage by an unseen hand. When he regained his balance, he swivelled from us to the corridor in bafflement before straightening up and adjusting his tie.

"How may I be of service, gentlemen?"

"It's McCavour," said Cuthbertson. "He's had a sudden attack."

"Of death," I explained.

Over the body, Selkirk was solemnly spinning his sixpence in hopes of illumination. The servant continued to await further information.

"We were wondering," said Milford, "what the club policy is for this sort of thing."

Billingsly visibly regirded himself in his customary butlerian aura. "I shall tend to the matter, gentlemen. A physician shall be summoned," he assured us, gesturing to the door to intimate that we should vacate the grisly scene for more pleasant chambers on the ground floor.

"Poor devil," said Cuthbertson, tapping some cigar ash onto McCavour's trousers before making for the exit. "Well, at least all that's sorted out, now. Could use a snifter of something. What do you say?"

Seeing McCavour lying there, a helpless victim of all-conquering mortality, had rather taken the impetus out of our investigative spirit, as such dour sights so often do, especially after a heavy meal. We filed out into the hall once more — Selkirk a trifle reluctantly — where I pointed out that we no longer had a waiter.

"Bound to be a decanter of something someplace," said Cuthbertson, the authority on finding a nice glass of something. "In the smoking room. The sideboard."

A certain amount of dispute ensued as to the appropriate liqueur for this particular stage of our interrupted meal, argument which had a deleterious effect on Selkirk's equanimity, but at least he did not resume divining with his sixpence. With one thing and another, though, we must have been walking down the corridor for nearly five minutes when, in a general, indefinable atmosphere of frustration, I noticed that we had not yet reached the stairs.

I stopped. The others stopped.

"A bit long, this hall, don't you think?"

Selkirk drew out his string again.

"I say," said Milford, who was examining a portrait between two doors on the left-hand wall. "What a handsome lady!"

We all, except Selkirk, clustered about the picture. It was, as Milford had noted, a quite striking young woman in a burgundy gown posed, Renaissance-fashion, leaning against a table laden with compasses, papers, cubes, and similar bric-a-brac.

"Fine lookin' filly. Looks a bit annoyed at somethin'," Cuthbertson commented. "But what're all those, you know, whattayacallums?"

"I say," Milford said again, rather unnecessarily. He leant closer, fixing the portrait with bulging, shiny eyes, obviously lovestruck in that gruesome manner one reads about in certain novels. Still, she *was* lovely.

"I fancy," I said, "that would be Maddox's cousin, Griggs. I remember him mentioning once that this was her house. Mathematician. A brilliant one, if I recall. Expert in higher mathematics."

"What, the whacking great numbers, you mean?" asked Cuthbertson. "Millions, and … and … tens of millions, and all that?"

"Well …"

"Pretty smile," noted Cuthbertson.

"I'd've sworn," Milford said, still ogling the painting, "I mean, there wasn't a smile a moment ago … was there?" He seemed to gather his senses. "Is she, you know …" He cleared his throat. "Married?"

Feeling sorry for the poor ninny, I patted him on the back. "I'm afraid she's dead, Milford. That's what I meant when I said this *was* her house. Maddox inherited it. Gave it over for the club, you see."

It was a hard blow for Milford. But a man who travels halfway 'round the globe, and then has the strength to eat durian fruit, is not easily daunted. Not even the raised eyebrow on the picture deterred him. The fire returned.

"But … all this spirit business. Mightn't she still be … how would one put it ... still *available?*"

"Good God, man," Cuthbertson exclaimed, choking on a puff of smoke, "she's dead, for heaven's sake!"

When he returned to me for an opinion, I had to nod gravely to Milford. "And more importantly, you should bear in mind that you're already married."

Milford's gaze fell back onto the painting, which I now saw had two raised eyebrows, and rather wide-open eyes.

"But surely," Milford said, lost in speculation, "Surely if your second wife is *already* dead ..."

A certain abstraction was occasioned by this Jesuitical piece of reasoning. It caused Cuthbertson's expression to twist like that of a viceroy presented with a particularly knotted-up yogi.

"Yes," I said. "Yes, I suggest you discuss the matter with the archbishop, Milford, before you do anything precipitate."

Selkirk chose this moment to intrude upon our contemplation of art and necrogamy.

"If you have quite finished ..." he said.

I flapped a hand to reassure Selkirk that we should follow his guidance in all things.

"As you seem to have already forgotten," he continued, leading us to the stairs, "McCavour's etheric form is yet abroad. There must be an immediate séance to establish contact."

"And send 'im packin'," said Cuthbertson. He waggled his cigar toward the ceiling. "Don't want my dinners interrupted every night by the silverware dancin' a pa-de-doo!"

Milford's hand rose to rub his larynx in sympathy with this sentiment.

"Ah," I said. "Now, better even than a séance," — and I really did not fancy the thought of passing the balance of the night holding hands in the dark with my erstwhile dining companions — "would be Maddox's machine. The Pneumatypograph, I believe he called it."

"Bloody sort of name," said Cuthbertson.

Our downward negotiation of the stairs was cut short when they seemed to contract, accordion-fashion, into a mere four or five steps, nearly propelling several of us into Pythagoras. We hastened thence to the library, except for Cuthbertson, who went to retrieve the smoking-room decanter. From one of the shelves I recovered the Pneumatypograph and arranged it on the main table.

"Hmm ... hmm," Selkirk muttered, examining the thing from various angles.

"Looks like one of those pomander things," said the returning Cuthbertson. "You know, oranges stuck full of cloves."

It did, a bit. Maddox's Pneumatypograph had a hemispherical dome bristling with lettered keys. A sliding tray beneath carried a curved sheet of paper that could be moved in and out of the machine by a lever in order to view the type-writing.

Selkirk quickly annexed the chair and the machine, running his fingers experimentally over the keys.

"You need to wear this blindfold," I told him, as I wrapped the black cloth about his eyes. "The spirit guides your fingers to the letters."

"Of course."

"Looks quite harmless, doesn't it? Not like that other thing Maddox made."

"Other ...?" asked Selkirk, turning eyelessly towards me.

"You know. That machine he made. The incident they talk about. At the twenty-seventh meeting."

Selkirk wrinkled his forehead and then jerked upright in the chair. He whisked off the cloth.

"Hmm. Everything seems in order here. Now I am ready to observe the operation, objectively, from ..." he said, moving quickly to the far end of the long table, "from here. Milford, be a good fellow and act as our medium."

"What incident?" asked Milford.

I held a beckoning hand towards the empty chair.

"Before your time, Milford."

"Ah." Milford installed himself.

I put the blindfold in place and guided Milford's hands to the device. When all was in order, we took our seats at the table.

"Whisky?" Cuthbertson offered.

"Yes, about three fingers, I should say," Milford agreed.

"Your fingers are occupied, Milford. Anybody else?"

Selkirk and I shook our heads. Cuthbertson shrugged, refilled his glass, and lit another cigar.

"All right, Lichfield," Selkirk said, "commence the séan- ... the ... proceedings."

I straightened my shoulders, and adjusted my *mien*.

"Allardyce McCavour..." I intoned.

"Allardyce ...!" exclaimed Cuthbertson.

"Shush. *Allardyce McCavour*, we beseech you to hear our questions, and communicate through our servant, ah, Milford, whom you already know, and through the medium of the Pneumatypograph. Come to us, and tell us of your passage to the etheric realm, and of why your rest is disturbed."

We sat impatiently in the ensuing silence. Milford had one ear cocked, as though listening for table-raps. A spasm ran through his little finger. Then his hands began to type.

"I say," said Milford, his fingers dancing madly over the sphere of keys. We all bent towards the machine, watching.

At a pause, I threw the paper-lever to view the result. The others clustered about.

I TRIED TO TELL YOU. I POINTED WITH THE CUTLERY. LED YOU WITH THE LIGHTS. USED THE MIRROR. BUT NO. YOU HAD TO RAMBLE ON ABOUT CHINESE STINK-BERRIES, TWIDDLE WITH SIXPENCES, AND ALL THE REST. NOW LOOK WHAT HAS HAPPENED.

Cuthbertson extracted his cigar and leant over to Milford's ear. "Awfully sorry about you snuffing it, old man, but really, you could have been more. You know. Clear."

"Stop shouting," complained Milford. "He's a ghost, you know, not a flea in my ear."

His hands went to the keys, necessitating a hasty return of the paper to its tray. When the typing ceased, I drew it out once more.

I AM NOT MCCAVOUR! MCCAVOUR WAS CHOKING ON A HUMBUG. I TRIED TO SUMMON HELP, BUT A LOT OF GOOD THAT DID. BY THE TIME YOU HAD MANAGED TO GET UPSTAIRS HE HAD HAD HEART FAILURE. WHAT I WANT TO KNOW IS HOW YOU ARE GOING TO EVICT HIM. I HAVE NO INTENTION OF SHARING MY HOUSE FOR ETERNITY WITH A SUPERANNUATED SPECTRE IN A

WALRUS MOUSTACHE.

"What's it say?" asked Milford.

"Do I," I said, "have the honour to be addressing Miss Bronwyn Havelock Griggs?"

"Bronwyn!" Milford whispered, reverently.

YOU DO.

"Well get McCavour on this thing," demanded Selkirk. "We're not here to chit-chat with Maddox's relations."

"Anyhow," said Cuthbertson, "McCavour's a member. Can't just throw him out into the street. Must be ε rule about it. Better ask the, you know. Thing. Custard."

"Custard?" said Milford.

Selkirk looked about ready to cradle his head and moan pitiably.

"Custa-rusta-whatsit," explained Cuthbertson.

"Ah," I said. "The *Custos Rotulorum*. I believe that would be I. No-one else wanted to be Keeper of the Rolls."

Milford aimed his blindfold in my direction. "Is that some sort of ceremonial waiter?"

"If I recall," I said, ignoring Milford, "club rules allow for expulsion in the event of misconduct. I hardly think, however, that choking on a humbug qualifies as misconduct. Not unless he stole the humbug from another member."

"'Course, McCavour's membership might have expired. When *he* did, I mean," suggested Cuthbertson.

Rules and precedents were little guide on this occasion, unfortunately.

"Ask McCavour why he has not moved on," suggested Selkirk, with the slow pedantry of an instructor of idiots.

YOU CANNOT. MCCAVOUR HAS NOT YET COALESCED INTO A COHERENT ETHERIC FORM.

"I suppose he has no place else to go," I suggested.

As we considered how to dispose of the immaterial remains of our fellow member, I felt the hair on my arms tingle and rise in gooseflesh. The gaslights flickered, and Cuthbertson's cigar fumes first swirled, then roiled like a summer cloud, condensing at last into a semblance of human form — into the likeness of Miss Bronwyn Griggs, her hands hovering translucently over Milford's.

"What is it?" asked Milford, perhaps hearing our collective intake of breath.

"Nothing... remain where you are," I told him. Griggs' eyes narrowed, and her fingers moved against his.

I THINK YOU WILL FIND THESE PREMISES QUITE UNSATISFACTORY, SHOULD I BE FORCED TO SHARE THEM WITH ANOTHER SPIRIT.

"Threats!" said Selkirk. "If it's an exorcism you want, I'll ..."

I waved Selkirk back into his chair

"Let me think," I said, temporizing. McCavour was a dull sort of cove for an eternal housemate, to be sure, but blameless enough. And it was probably quite true that he had nowhere else to go, or to haunt.

"I should like to propose that we confirm McCavour's membership. As a perpetual *resident* member."

The others all gabbled at once in response, with Griggs typing furiously until I held a hand up for silence.

"It would be ill-mannered in the extreme to simply evict a member who so recently suffered the loss of both his livelihood, and his life. As a member, McCavour is subject to club authority. Should he, through any misbehaviour," I said, looking to Miss Griggs, "transgress the standards of the club, he will be subject to a termination of membership. Which, I hardly need mention, would require *immediate* expulsion from the club premises."

The other members pondered this. Even Griggs looked thoughtful.

I SUPPOSE THAT WOULD BE ACCEPTABLE.

"Let us vote on it, then, and be done with it," said Selkirk. "If we have quorum."

"What's *quorum?*" inquired Cuthbertson.

Milford cleared his throat and looked around blindly. "I think there's a dictionary in here, someplace."

"Oh, God," moaned Selkirk. "I'm going home. Good night!"

With which, he departed.

"As *Custos Rotulorum*, I declare there to be no quorums in the Etheric Explorers Club," I said.

"Good," said Cuthbertson. "Didn't like the sound of 'em, these *quorums*."

"And furthermore," I continued, "I should like to propose that Miss Bronwyn Griggs be elected a Fellow, in perpetuity, of the Etheric Explorers Club."

Cuthbertson chuckled around his cigar. "The rest of 'em'll have fits when we tell 'em we elected a woman."

WHAT?

"As a great benefactress of the club, as a scholar, and …" I said, enjoying Griggs' full attention, "… and as an individual with a unique insight into the etheric realm, Miss Griggs is an admirable candidate for membership. And, as a Fellow, she will enjoy seniority over McCavour."

"Agreed," said Cuthbertson.

"Agreed!" added Milford.

"Very well, the resolution is passed. Congratulations, Miss Griggs."

A FELLOW?

"Now, I think we've imposed upon Miss Griggs enough for one day," I concluded, and stood to wave away the smoke-figure before Milford could wrestle off his blindfold.

Cuthbertson frowned in what I, for a dreadful moment, interpreted as an unexpected burst of ratiocination culminating in objection. Then, I understood that it was the empty decanter which was provoking his wrath. He drained the last of his whiskey and heaved himself to his feet, stubbing out his cigar.

"Well, that's that," he said, rather as I imagined Wellington summing up affairs after the clouds of gun-smoke parted to reveal no more Frenchmen standing on the field of Waterloo. "Time to be getting home, I suppose."

Taking my hint, if reluctantly, Milford arose, flexing his fingers thoughtfully. "Well, good night, Lichfield. Miss Griggs …" he said, searching about for any signs of a continued presence. A look of hope, or desperation, passed across his phiz. "I wonder ... should Miss Griggs be not otherwise engaged tomorrow, if I might inquire as to whether she, er ..."

I placed my hand upon his shoulder in a kindly way, dropping into a confidential whisper. "Miss Griggs has had a trying ordeal tonight, Milford. I know I can rely upon your considerate, chivalrous nature to allow her that peaceful solitude which is the greatest balm for a troubled soul."

"Of course! I didn't mean to, you know ... as you say."

"Damned right," said Cuthbertson, adding a rather elaborate wink in my direction while Milford was busy stuttering out further protests. "Let's be off."

For a few minutes after Cuthbertson had escorted our medium away, I meditated upon the evening's extraordinary events. Then, when I was certain the others had collected their coats and found cabs, I turned the key in the library door before seating myself by the Pneumatypograph and slipping the blindfold on.

It seemed I was in a dark room, shared by I knew not what. Perhaps Griggs. Perhaps nothing. Perhaps things yet unimagined. Certainly I tried not to imagine them as I waited. Then a tickle on the arm. A draught of air? No. A tingling. A pair of hands, delicate, covered mine with the softest touch imaginable, gentler than any flesh. My fingers moved unbidden, the machine tak-tak-takking, until the message ceased. I removed the mask.

THANK-YOU. I THINK. BY THE WAY, THE BLINDFOLD IS NOT NECESSARY. RAFE ONLY INCLUDED IT FOR THE SAKE OF OBJECTIVITY.

On a whim, I relit Cuthbertson's cigar, placing it in the ashtray, and my hands back upon the machine. With the delightful sensation of their enclosure by Griggs' own came the misty likeness, forming from the tobacco smoke.

"I ..." Trembling slightly, I began again. "I read your paper on Riemannian surfaces, in *Acta Mathematica*. It seemed to suggest very radical ideas about the dimensions of space, and even about time," I said, remembering now some of the curious phenomena from earlier in the evening. "Though, not being a mathematician, I failed to grasp much of the matter of it. Have you ever ... applied your theories?"

POSSIBLY. BUT IT IS SO DIFFICULT TO WORK, BEING UN-ABLE TO HANDLE A BOOK OR WRITE, EXCEPT CRUDELY AND WITH GREAT EFFORT. PERHAPS WITH PRACTICE.

"If I can be of any service, please call upon me at any hour to turn your page, or hold your pen. It is the least I can do, my dear lady, after we have encumbered you with a phantom McCavour."

TO BE PERFECTLY HONEST, MR LICHFIELD, I MAY NOT BE ENTIRELY INNOCENT IN THAT REGARD. WHEN MY SUMMONSES WERE NOT PROMPTLY ANSWERED, I AM AFRAID I APPEARED IN MCCAVOUR'S MIRROR, HOPING TO STARTLE HIM INTO EXPELLING THE SWEET. AS YOU KNOW, SHOCKS CAN BE EFFECTIVE AT REMEDYING HICCOUGHS AND THUS IT SEEMED REASONABLE THAT THE SAME MIGHT BE TRUE FOR CHOKING. THE SHOCK WAS, PERHAPS, TOO MUCH FOR MCCAVOUR'S HEART. HENCE THE C A R D I O I D.

"Please, call me Cedric."

BRONWYN.

"Dear Bronwyn, you mustn't blame yourself. McCavour lived well, and came to an honourable end."

DO YOU KNOW, CEDRIC, WHAT I MISS MORE EVEN THAN MY WORK?

"What is that?"

A GOOD RUBBER OF WHIST.

I leapt up and rummaged through one of the library drawers.
"Here is the deck. I hesitate to call in Billingsly and our chef to bring us up to the required four, but if you could settle for écarté, and promise not to look at my cards, I will be yours until dawn."

About the Author

PAUL MARLOWE'S SHORT fiction has been published around the world. The steampunk collection *Ether Frolics* is representative of this international popularity, containing stories that first appeared in magazines in the United Kingdom, Australia, the United States, and South Africa, as well as previously unpublished stories.

His teen steampunk series *The Wellborn Conspiracy*, set in 1880s Nova Scotia, has received widespread critical approval; the first volume in the series, *Sporeville*, was included in *Resource Links* magazine's Year's Best list for 2007, and the sequel, *Knights of the Sea*, has been called "drily hilarious" (Kelly Lasiter, *fantasyliterature.com*), "a fast-paced blend of action-adventure, fantasy and historical novel, with the added elements of erudition, humour and wit" (Ruth Latta, *CM Magazine*), and "Fun reading that will delight fans of Phillip Pullman" (Lois McNicol, *TriState Reviews*). The radio play produced of his short story "The Resident Member" has been broadcast on radio stations in Canada and the United States, and was called an "instant classic" by Sonic Society.

For more about the author and his work, visit his website at:
www.paulmarlowe.com